WHEN DOG DAYS WEPT

BENJAMIN BISHOP

For Chelsea

Table of Contents

PART ONE

ENDINGS AND BEGINNINGS

CHAPTER 1

Opening his eyes, the boy stared at nothing and everything all at once, the overhead fan casting murderous shadows across the room, falling on the boy's sullen face. He was lying on his bed, not with his arms behind his head like he usually did, but instead his arms were stiff at his sides like he was a corpse. Except he wasn't. At least not yet anyways. He had been lying that way, for how long he didn't really know, listening to his breath and the monotonous hum of the air conditioner. He wanted nothing more than to stay in this position forever, and maybe he would, watching the days drift passed like clouds dissolving away into the great abyss of nothingness that was all around him now. Days turning into months and then eventually into years, where all he did was sink further into that darkness and then finally into emptiness, and then if he was lucky enough, becoming nothing himself.

Laughter came from outside his bedroom window. Other kids were playing nearby. A girl screamed and then began to giggle. He could hear their voices grow louder as they approached on their bikes, or maybe they were on skateboards, and then he listened as their voices faded away as they rode passed his house. Somewhere nearby, a dog began to bark and then howl. It was funny, but not really, how not even a week ago he would have been outside laughing and playing too.

One week ago everything had been the same.

But not anymore.

Summer had always been his favorite time of the year, and not just because he was out of school for ten weeks, that was only part of why he loved the season so much, but the real reason was that he was able to be outside from sunup to sundown riding his bike all day long, each turn of his pedals taking him on a new adventure that only he could write across dirt and asphalt, trying to escape each day's coming sunset, and then when it finally did catch him, playing outside under the warm moon and rising stars until the streetlights came on, signaling him home for the night, just to do it all over again the next day.

But now, summer would always be a reminder of him.

The boy rolled onto his side, sighing deeply.

When his parents moved into the four bedroom, Ranch-style home on Maple Street in the spring of '82, Theodore Stafford had only been a glimmer in his young mother's eye, a glimmer Meredith Stafford had been dreaming of ever since she was a child herself and was still known by the name of little

Mary Downer. She was eighteen when she married James Stafford, her high school sweetheart, and she was nineteen when Theodore was born. When Mary had told James that she wanted kids, and lots of them, he said they needed a house first. He enlisted in the U.S. Army a week later and then they used his VA home loan to purchase their home in Grand View, California, the same city they had both lived in their entire lives, and the only home Theodore had ever known.

Not only would summer now always be a reminder of him, but everywhere he turned in the house, there was the specter of him staring back as if their home had become an inescapable mausoleum forever memorializing the life they would never have again. And they were now the ghosts left behind to wander. Forgotten relics. Consecrated by his last act.

"Teddy?"

A knock came at his bedroom door. He didn't respond.

"Teddy, it's mom. I'm coming in."

Of course it was mom.

There was no one else it could be.

He still said nothing.

The door opened, and she walked into the room. He could feel her eyes staring at him, and he could feel her contemplating what to do and what to say next. He could feel her words getting stuck in her throat, words that had been so easy and so natural for her to speak mere days before were now the furthest thing from both of those things. Nothing was easy anymore, and not a goddamn thing was even in the same ballpark as natural.

She sat down at the end of the bed, reaching her hand out toward him but stopped, putting her hands in her lap instead. Her disheveled sandy-blonde hair hung in wisps across her face. She pushed the strands of hair behind her ears and then gripped her hands in her lap again.

"Teddy," she paused. He could feel her thinking. Debating which words to choose to make this better, except no words could ever make this better. At least not for a very long time anyways. "I think it's time that you went outside."

He wished she would go outside and just leave him alone.

"Summer is almost half over." She gripped her hands harder, twisting them nervously. "If you stay in here, you'll miss the whole thing."

Still he said nothing.

She sighed and stood.

"Well, at least come downstairs and have some breakfast."

She walked to the door and held the knob in her hand, turning back to look at her son, pursing her lips. Even with his back to her, she couldn't help but to notice how much Teddy resembled him. Now, strangers passing by on the streets would no longer remark at how similar their eyes were when they furrowed their brows at the setting sun, turning them from a hazy green to a stormy blue, and no one would mention how they both had the same contemplative look when they were deep in thought at the coffee shop as they read over the menu, even though they both always ended up ordering the same thing. It would only be photographs holding onto those secrets now, and eventually even those began to dim and grow yellow. A memory can last a lifetime, and sometimes longer, if a person is really lucky, but most of the time it's only scars that truly stick around. But given enough time, those fade as well.

After she left the room, Teddy lay for a moment more, staring at the rotating fan overhead, and then he sat up. He rubbed his hand under his eyes, a habit he had picked up over the last few days, but there was nothing there to wipe away. The tears had dried up, leaving an empty hole instead.

He walked into the kitchen and his mom was standing at the counter with her back to him. The smell of coffee hung in the air, thick and bitter. She was silently crying, he could tell because her shoulders were shaking up and down, but she quickly stopped when she heard him walk in.

"Breakfast?" She turned, mug of coffee in hand. Her eyes were a pink-red like the rising sun creeping in through the bay windows behind her.

"Not hungry."

Teddy walked over to the kitchen table and sat down at his normal spot across from where his mom always sat. It was a small rectangular table made of mahogany with six matching chairs. There had been a spot for each of them, plus three extra. But now it would be just the two of them, making the usually small feeling table feel suddenly too big for just the both of them. He hung his head, his shaggy brownish-blonde hair like drapes over his eyes, staring at the place at the table where he had found it.

The letter.

"You know it's not your fault, right?"

"I know."

His eyes not moving, hiding behind his hair.

"And you know that there was nothing you could do to make him stay?"

"I know."

He didn't want to start crying again, he had done enough of that, but he could annoyingly feel the tears coming behind his eyes like a warm evening tide.

"Your dad was—" She paused, thinking. "Your dad was sick, that's all. He just never let on to either of us that he was."

He stared for a moment longer at the place where he had found the letter, then pushed himself away from the table and stood, making his chair topple backwards and clatter to the floor. His eyes flashed violently like a coming storm.

"Sick people go to a doctor." He glared at her.

She stared quietly, twisting her hands again.

"They don't do what he did," Teddy said.

She was startled at how different his voice sounded. Somehow older and raspier like sandpaper. Meaner even. She had never known him to act this way. In fact, she had even gone as far as to believe that Teddy didn't have a mean bone in his body. His teachers at school were always complimenting him, saying how he was always smiling and so polite and how he was kind to other students, and the few times that kindness had not been received well by some of the other kids and Teddy would be picked on, getting called names like *goody two shoes* or *suck-up* or *brown-noser*, he had always brushed off those other kids like he didn't have a care in the world. She couldn't help it, but the way his voice sounded now, slightly worried her.

"It's okay to be upset."

He didn't say anything.

"And it's even okay to be angry."

He stared at her, looked over at the spot where the letter had been left, then looked back at her again. She could see tears building in his eyes.

"I'm angry too," she said.

The tears began to fall from his eyes, running down his cheeks. She was also crying. She wanted to go to him, to hold him in her arms, but she knew better. She had to wait for him to come to her. If she went to him now, she could lose him for good, and that scared her even more than the anger in her son's voice. She had already lost one man in her life, she wasn't sure if she could bear to lose another. Moments like these did not come often in a young boy's life, but the results could forever determine the path leading them toward the future man they would become one day.

They stood that way, crying in the kitchen as the sun rose over the horizon, rays of light growing across the kitchen like the chasm that was slowly growing between mother and son. She could feel him leaving her, feel him wanting to go, just as her husband had gone, but still she held her ground. She wouldn't make the same mistake twice. She folded her arms across her chest and waited.

"It's not fair."

"I know." She nodded her head, but kept her place.

"He wasn't supposed to go."

"I know."

She knew this had to happen now, or it may never happen again. She bit her lower lip, tasting metal in her mouth. She unfolded her arms, then folded them again, digging her nails into her skin. Leaving marks. Red crescent moons across her arms.

He looked at the door.

She saw the internal struggle inside of him ragging like a wildfire that couldn't be contained, and watched helplessly, waiting to see which path her son would take, a decision every boy becoming a man must chose at least once in his lifetime, determining the course of one's life and the linchpin of all future events thereafter.

"I hate him."

"I know."

His fists were clenched.

"I hate him."

"I know," she whispered.

She nodded again, crying harder because she knew that in the next moment, her son could be lost to her forever.

"But I miss him so much too."

Teddy sobbed. His shoulders slackened, and he hung his head.

She watched as the moment passed. Teddy's fists loosened, and then she sighed deeply. She was shaking. She had not lost him. He was still hers. She knew he would choose correctly, but he had to be the one who made the decision.

"I miss him so much. Why did he leave me? Why did he leave us?"

The words that had been locked inside of him all week came spilling out like an angry ocean.

She opened her arms and he came to her. She embraced him as only a mother can, stroking his hair as he cried into her bosom. They stayed that way, the sun changing from a reddish-orange to a blinding white, until the moment had passed, but she would hold onto that moment for years to come, standing there in the kitchen, remembering how she had almost lost him as well, but then remembering how it had all worked out in the end, like it always seems to do even when there seems to be no coming rider bringing good news on the horizon. She held him, and he allowed her to kiss his forehead, something she probably wouldn't be able to do for much longer, and the faint hint of a smile began on the corner of her lips, and then passed as quickly as it had begun to form.

And then they sat down at the table, just the two of them now for a long while, and had breakfast.

He walked into the garage, the door creaking behind him as it closed shut. Teddy stood for a moment, uneasy but not scared, which he felt he should be. Instead, it was as if he were entering a sacred space, a place holding power because his father often dwelt here.

He reached against the wall for the garage opener and pressed the button. The garage door rumbled open like the stone the angels rolled away from the messiah's tomb he had learned about in Sunday school class, letting the disciples know he had gone away. His consecrated shroud the only indication he had ever been concealed inside, and the angels declaring to his followers that they had been duped, or something along those lines. Teddy couldn't really remember, because his parents had stopped going to church when his father had returned from his tour over in a desert Teddy couldn't remember the name of either. What he did remember was his father had been gone for over six months, even missing Teddy's eighth birthday. When Teddy had asked his father what the name of the place was that he had gone to fight in was called, his father told him that it didn't matter. "Lots of dirt and sand," was what his father had told him. "And hotter and sweatier than a whore sitting in the front pew at church on a Sunday morning. Probably dirtier too."

Teddy felt like he was in a tomb now, standing in the silence of the garage.

This was his father's place.

The place where Teddy had found him.

And there were no angels here.

Often, Teddy would find him out here building something out of wood, a piece of furniture he would spend hours perfecting to then take down to the Friday market night that ran from Orange Street all the way down to Mt. Vernon Ave., and which was held once a week in the summer and then every other week as it began to cool down in the fall. He would go out there with his pop up canopy tent and two or three pieces of the furniture he had been working on and sometimes he would come back empty handed, but pockets full of cash.

Sometimes Teddy would find him working on his truck, socket wrench in one hand and beer in the other as he toiled away for hours on end. He always seemed to be working on the truck, so much so that Teddy wondered if his father really knew what he was doing out there in the garage, but he must have because the truck always ended up running when his father was finished tinkering around on it.

Other times his father would just come out here to think, and Teddy would find him at his workbench, not necessarily doing anything at all. There had been a few incidences where Teddy had come out to the garage to see his father crouched down or hunched over and staring at a knot in the wood, as if he had discovered a crooked eye hidden within the grain that he was trying to gleam some ancient wisdom from. Teddy would watch his father, unmoving, and a chill would run down his back as his father stood there looking at nothing.

Teddy sat down on the cement stair that led into the house. He grabbed his pair of black Converse high-tops that were sitting by the door and slipped them on. As he tied his shoes, he glanced around the garage.

He had not been out here since the incident.

He saw one of his father's checkered hankies lying on the work bench against the side of the garage. A few tools were still sitting out as well, and the little desk lamp that his father used for extra light, was still on. Teddy walked over to the bench and flicked off the lamp. He picked up the hammer and then put it back in his father's standing metal tool box next to the workbench and then began putting away the cluster of nails and the handsaw. Sawdust hung in the air like a light fog as he moved and put away the tools. A chair leg that his father had been sanding, lay atop the bench. Teddy always loved the smell of the freshly shaved wood from the sandpaper. Looking around at the mess, it was as if his father had only been here moments before.

Teddy picked up the red and white cloth that his father would normally keep in his back pocket, using it to wipe the sweat from off his brow. Teddy held it to his nose for a moment, the sent still fresh and lingering, and then put it into his own back pocket.

His father had left a reminder too, that he had gone away from his sacred place.

Teddy saw his metallic blue bike, propped against its kickstand on the opposite side of the garage. Hanging from one of the handlebars was his little league baseball cap, dark blue and sweat stained. He walked over, threw one leg over the seat, and then sat down, feeling the rubber handlebar grips in his hands once again. He had almost forgotten how good it could feel to sit on a bike, especially during the summer when all there was to do was ride until your legs felt like they would just about fall off. He grabbed his hat from off the handlebars and pulled it onto his head, rolling the bill inward.

The sun was now almost fully up, and he stared out at the asphalt street, beckoning him to go on one more ride passed the horizon to a place where only summertime children could ride because there was nothing to call them back until the moon had come up on the other side and the stars reminded them it was time to turn around, lighthouses in the sky guiding them home once again.

He looked up at the wooden beams that ran across the top of the garage, his eyes landing on the one higher up than the rest. He could still see him, swinging there, slowly twisting from the creaking rope around his neck. His face looked swollen and bruised like he had jumped headfirst into a nest of angry hornets, and his tongue was hanging from the corner his mouth.

Teddy pushed the kickstand of his bike back with his left heel, gripping the handlebars tightly again, and then he rode toward the horizon and the rising sun.

CHAPTER 2

It felt good to be on his bike again. Natural. Like how it was supposed to be. He rode into the city just as the last golden streaks of the sun had finished reaching over the horizon, guiding him on the path ahead to where the day stood waiting for him to come meet it. He breathed in the cool air, feeling the warmth of the sun on his arms and face. A few crows cawed overhead, perched atop a sleeping streetlight. They turned and watched as he rode underneath them and headed downtown.

The city was beginning to wake up, and a few cars drove passed him as he rode across the street and onto the sidewalk. One of the cars, a brown Chrysler as big as a boat, honked at Teddy and then a hand came out the driver's window and waved. Teddy waved back and kept on his way.

He rode his bike down Mt. Vernon Ave., by several buildings of various heights, each casting shadows across the sidewalk, his own shadow playing hide-and-seek in front of him. A few large Victorian houses were intermixed within the buildings, relics of a forgotten era. The large homes stood on even larger corner lots with black iron rod fences and extravagant lawn decorations. Some of them, still very much homes where families dwelt, whereas others now served as offices for accountants and lawyers. A man with a thick white moustache, wearing a grey newsie cap and matching suspenders, was sweeping the sidewalk in front of a second hand clothing shop. He stopped as Teddy rode passed on his bike and then continued sweeping.

Across the street, in front of a shop simply called *Donuts* with red and gold alternating letters on the sign, a woman wearing a hairnet and an apron was spraying off the sidewalk with a hose. The smell of wet concrete hung in the air, mixing with the fresh sweet smells of the bakery. Teddy's stomach rumbled, even though he had already eaten breakfast that morning with his mother. He turned his handlebars and headed in the direction of the donut shop, riding over the curb of the sidewalk and then popping a wheelie up the other side. He leaned his bike up against the brick building beside the entryway into the shop and rolled the brim of his baseball cap inward as he walked toward the door. Through the large picture window of the storefront, Teddy could see several people sitting down at some of the booths inside.

"Good morning." Teddy said.

The woman smiled up at him, crow's feet fanning out around her eyes. She was slightly shorter than Teddy was.

"Morning," she said back, continuing to spray the sidewalk.

He pushed open the glass door and a three-chimed bell greeted him as he walked inside. The smell of fresh coffee and warm pastries lingered. A girl with black pigtails, sitting at a booth with her mother, smiled at him as he walked by. She had rainbow sprinkles stuck to her cheeks. Teddy walked up to the counter, examining the various pastries.

"Can I please get one chocolate bar?"

"Sure thing," replied the heavyset man behind the counter, wearing the white paper hat. "You want a bag?"

"Yes, please."

"That will be forty cents."

"And a carton of milk too, please."

"Twenty-five cents more."

Teddy reached into his pocket and dug out three quarters, handing them across the glass counter to the man.

"Keep the change," Teddy said, grabbing the white bag and his carton of milk and then headed back outside.

The woman spraying the sidewalk had disappeared. Teddy looked for a dry spot and then sat down on the curb, putting the bag and carton down next to him. A light breeze ran down the street making a few leaves twirl across to the other side where they eventually lay still in the gutter. Exhaust wafted from cars passing by. Teddy pulled the donut out of the bag beside him and took a bite, smiling. Warm chocolate dripped down his chin. He finished the donut in four bites and then opened the carton of milk, washing every last crumb down. He put the carton into the bag, crumbled it, and then tossed it into the trashcan next to the front door of the shop.

He hoped on his bike and peddled down Mt. Vernon Ave., turning right, up Main Street. He rode passed buildings that had stood since the late 1800s when the city was still just a town and was established in the spring of 72' on a dusty plot of ground, where all there had been were a few tumbleweeds and a field full of Russian thistle and spurge, and instead the mayor and the city council voting to replace it with rows and rows of orange trees which started the town down the path to becoming the orange capital of America, planted by Mexican migrant workers, cultivating and fertilizing soil and land their ancestors had once owned. Migrants in a foreign land even though they had never left.

Eventually though, as progress rolled through the town of Grand View and the town naturally grew into a city and more buildings and houses were built, the orange groves became less and less predominant. However, the city still held strong to the culture that had been established many years before, and the new mayor and city council voted to make the orange the icon of the city, plastering it on everything from street signs to window fronts, and even going as far as to put orange shipment containers on the corner of every busy street as a reminder to the city's historic roots.

Teddy passed the police station where a couple of patrolman sat leaning against their cruiser. Each was holding a Styrofoam cup of coffee in their hand. One nodded to Teddy as he wheeled passed and Teddy nodded back, continuing on his way down Main Street passed the barber shop where his mom would take him once a month to get his haircut. The spinning barber pole sign alternating between a spiraling red, white, and blue.

As the morning led him forward, he found his way riding through Grant Park, going by the Mexican-American War monuments. The bronze statues of brave men watched as he weaved his way across the grass and in-between the various Jacaranda trees whose bright purple flowers filled the sky above and dusted the ground below creating an aromatic scent that only nature herself could formulate, unbeknownst to him that the lawn he rode through had once been foreign ground to those who now claimed it as home, and where if the ground were to speak, it would cry out that the earth had for centuries before been trodden upon by a people deemed enemies by the intruders who had eventually secured the land for themselves, and that the trees he rode beneath had been planted by those same hands, and the fallen flowers now served as purple hearts for those who had lost their land.

Crossing through the park, Teddy rode down a grassy hill and dropped his bike. A small lake stood before him. He walked around the lake, the sun reflecting off the water sending prisms of reds and blues, a kaleidoscope of colors like tiny bursts of fire that only happened when the sun hit the water just right. Several water lilies floated across the still lake sitting atop dark green lily pads.

He walked around the lake, gathering small rocks, but not too small, black and grey, smooth and slender if he was lucky. Patches of clover with small pink flowers grew up around the base of the lake and a few Mallard ducks were enjoying their morning meal. A handful more were swimming through the water, sending small currents rippling out behind them. Several sycamore trees intermixed with a few large oaks surrounded the lake, ancient sentinels casting grey shadows out over the water and around the grassy knoll in scattered patches.

After he had what he thought was the correct amount of rocks, Teddy walked back toward his bike and set the rocks onto the ground in a small pile. He squatted down a foot or so from the water, forearms resting against his knees, and then took one of the stones in hand, feeling it between his fingers, then turned his hand sideways and with a flick of his wrist, sent the rock sailing across the top of the water. The smooth stone skipped several times across the water before it sunk below the disturbed water. Teddy grabbed another rock in hand and repeated the same motion with his wrist. This one skipped across the lake five times before it too sunk beneath. His record was nine skips.

His father had taught him how to skip rocks.

His record had been eleven.

It had started with taking Teddy out to the lake to feed the ducks. Each week, sometimes more maybe, when Teddy's mother noticed that the bread bag was getting low and all that was left were the heels that no one wanted to eat, she would tell her husband that it was time to go feed the ducks. Teddy would always squeal with delight when he would hear his mother make this declaration from within the kitchen pantry, and he would walk around the kitchen repeating *duck, duck, duck*. Teddy's father would pick him up and load him into the truck, and three of them would head down to Grant Park where they would spend the morning together throwing crumbs of bread into the water. Teddy would watch eagerly as the bread grew swollen and soggier by the second as the weight of the water began to pull the bloated bread down, and then he would laugh as a duck came darting over to gobble up the moist treat.

He stood up and began to toss the remainder of the rocks haphazardly across the lake, splashing the peaceful water like angry raindrops. Some of the ducks darted quickly away, running up the muddy shoreline, but a few brave ones merely floated to the other side. A dragonfly sped within the water lilies and another followed behind. They hovered for a moment and then left just as quickly as they had arrived.

Teddy walked up the grassy hill beside the lake. He sat down with his legs out before him, feet crossed, and leaned back against his elbows, watching the lake. He sat forward and took off his hat, setting it down on the grass beside him, feeling the cool morning breeze in his hair. He picked at the grass for a moment until he found a long piece suited to his liking and then put it in his mouth like a dead cigarette. He chewed on it for a while and then tossed it down the hill. He ran his hand through the grass, picked another long piece with a seed head on the end of it, and then began to chew on it too.

Down the hill at the playground, a mother was pushing a stroller while two young girls ran ahead of her. They were both laughing and one was chasing the other. The one being chased tripped and fell, rolling in the grass, and the other, out of solidarity, also tripped and began to roll along with her. Their mother pushed the stroller next to a wooden bench and sat down. A baby began to cry, and Teddy watched as the mother lifted her from the stroller and began to bounce the baby upon her knee.

A Great White Egret landed on the water, taking Teddy's attention away from the mother and the children playing down at the playground. The bird stood upon its two long legs, resembling the willow reeds that were growing up from out of the water, and began to walk through the shallow murky pond, slowly taking deliberate steps as it scanned the water, head turning quickly in every direction, looking for an unsuspecting carp or bass swimming near enough to be swallowed up.

Teddy got back on his bike and headed further up the hill, taking a winding dirt path that spiraled up and around, choking the hill. He passed a few wooden benches with no one on them and continued pedaling. The dusty road was littered with leaves and a few white petals from flowers that had been blown off the surrounding citrus trees. He rode his bike over several dry seed pods that had been dropped from the ancient palm trees scattered along the mud cracked road that continued to lead him further up the hill, the trees standing guard like waiting soldiers.

When he finally reached his destination, he hoped off and wheeled his bike the rest of the way to another wooden bench, sitting desolate and lonely, weathered and worn from the beating sun, a crack like a gully running down the seat of the bench. Teddy laid his bike on the ground and then took a seat on the bench. From this high up, he could see the whole valley below him, stretching miles and miles out before him, rolling hills and open plains, patches of green from trees that looked like islands floating in a desert wasteland. To the south he could see Riverside, the unofficial gateway to Anaheim and Los Angeles County where he would sometimes go to catch a baseball game with his parents, and to the west he saw the small towns of Loma Linda, Colton, Bloomington, and if he squinted hard enough, he could even make out Rialto, small cities he had only heard of and only seen from a distance. To the north lay San Bernardino National Forest where he had gone camping once with his father and had learned to fish and pitch a tent. His father had been so proud of him when he pulled a two foot trout from out of the river and had promised they would go back every summer. Two weeks later his father had been shipped out to the other side of the world, and when he had come back, his father had never mentioned camping or fishing again.

Broken promises etched into the fissures of a cracked heart.

Teddy scanned the land before him, like father Abraham had done in the story he had learned about in church, when God had led Abraham atop the mountain to show him the promised land. Except God had been there with Abraham, fellowshipping with him. Sharing in sacred communion. Teddy looked around and suddenly felt very alone. Thousands of people living their lives, each with a story to tell, and none of them even knowing he was staring down at them. He wondered, if God was real, what he would say to him, then figured he wouldn't say much, since God was God and all, and he was just a boy, and figured God probably had more important things to do than sit atop a hill and talk to him.

He wished his father was with him now, sitting atop the dirt hill on the cracked bench, so that he could talk to him one more time.

Nearby, a Red-Tailed Hawk circled overhead. A warm breeze passed through the trees behind him and the smell of citrus floated passed like a spray of perfume. The sound of the wind like the rising and falling tide of an ocean blew over the mountain.

He thought back to a time long ago when he was six-years-old, perhaps seven, when he had gone with his father to the home improvement store that sat between Main Street and Washington Ave, near the video store he would go to on the weekends. They had needed some new sprinkler heads that had busted off, probably from kids in the neighborhood who would sometimes go around stepping on the ones that were still popped up, making them spray water and unfortunately break at the same time. As they pulled into the parking lot of the store in his father's old blue pickup truck with the rusted chrome bumper, Teddy noticed a group of men standing off to the side of the entrance all dressed the same in embroidered button down shirts, faded blue jeans, and wearing dusty brown cowboy boots and either a matching cowboy hat or no hat at all. Some had short black hair, sweaty and greasy, and a couple had long hair tied in a thick black braid that ran down their backs. Skin like leather. Tired and worn like their jeans.

"Who are those men?"

"What men?"

"The ones standing over there."

Teddy's father looked toward the direction Teddy had pointed and nodded. "Those are the day laborers."

"Day laborers?" Teddy scrunched his face, confused.

"They are workers. Men you can hire to do odd jobs around your house."

"Like the jobs you do?"

Teddy's father chuckled, and then he nodded. "Yeah, sort of like me."

"Who pays them?"

"The people who hire them pay them."

"What happens if no one has any odd jobs for them to do?"

"Then they starve."

Teddy looked at the men, then he looked back at his father. "Could we maybe hire them to do some odd jobs around our house? Maybe they could fix the sprinklers."

His father was quiet for a moment. Stoic. They sat watching the men, engine idling, making the truck rumble and shake. "Come on, Teddy."

They climbed out of the truck, the door creaking like an angry bird call. Teddy walked around to his father's side of the truck and then followed him toward the men. They all turned and looked at him and the ones who had been sitting stood up, and they formed a line as if meeting a battalion leader.

Teddy's father examined the men, looking them over until his eyes met one man who looked to be about the same age as he was. He called the man over.

"Do you have any kids?'

"Sí. Yes. Two."

"Do you want to make some money today?"

"Sí. Yes."

"Good."

Teddy's father reached into his back pocket and pulled out his faded leather wallet that looked like it had seen better days. He opened it and then handed the man a one hundred dollar bill.

"I want you to go home and take your two kids out for some ice-cream. Take them down to the Thrifty's and get them two scoops each."

The man looked confused and pushed the money away.

"No, gracias. Only take money for trabajar. For work."

Teddy's father looked down at Teddy and then back at the man.

"That's the job I'm hiring for. You want that I hire someone else?"

The man looked back at the other day laborers, they were all watching, and then he shook his head. "No, señor.

"Good. Then it's settled."

Teddy's father held out the bill and the man took it slowly as if he expected it to bite him or that Teddy's father was playing a cruel joke on him and that he would suddenly pull it away, and when he realized that neither was going to happen, he smiled, dry cracked skin that looked like clay, and then he tilted his ranchero hat in appreciation.

Teddy stood, watching the busy valley below. A few stinging tears rolled down his cheeks and he knew that neither his father nor God could travel this road with him now.

There was no father up here on the hilltop with him. And no God either, for that matter.

He was all alone.

Teddy wondered how his father, who was so kind and caring to others, couldn't find it in his own heart to be kind to himself, and he figured he would never know the answer now.

After the moment passed, Teddy got on his bike and then headed back down the path. He twisted and turned down the road, an uncoiling serpent, his handle bars rumbling and making his fingers tingle like they had fallen asleep, until eventually the dirt turned back into asphalt, taking him back toward the city.

He rode down the sidewalk passed buildings where people were now coming and going, not thinking about anything but the bike beneath him and the street in front of him. If he could, he would ride all day, pedaling into the sunset and then beyond to where dreams could come true and where everything could become new again. He pushed down harder, wheels spinning beneath him, and raced down the street wishing that if he just pedaled hard enough, maybe perhaps he could make it to the great beyond where sunsets went to, and maybe he could even bring back old sunsets, ones that he and his father could sit and watch together.

Every young boy growing toward adulthood yearns to be the facsimile of their father, eventually surpassing them to become even greater than the original, but when the image of the father becomes tarnished, what remains is only an apparition, destitute and impoverished, forced to wander alone.

Teddy turned the corner down the street and then lifted his wheels onto the sidewalk. He turned another corner and then another and then stopped, nearly toppling over the handlebars. On the opposite side of the street he saw them. They were on their bikes. All three of them were there, and they saw him too. The Belfour Three, as they were known around the town.

He had forgotten all about them and understandably so. His mind had been preoccupied with his father, and he had made what could potentially turn out to be a grave mistake.

But they had not forgotten about him.

Teddy watched as they crossed the street and began to ride toward him, and then he turned on his bike and fled.

CHAPTER 3

He wondered how he could have been so stupid. He peddled frantically down the street, as if the devil himself were after him, knowing that he was a dead man.

He glanced over his shoulder, his hair sticking to his forehead like wet straw. He turned forward again and quickly swerved the handlebars, almost connecting straight into the backend of an old rusted Chevy pickup. It wouldn't have been the first time he had run into something while trying to get away from them.

"We're going to get you!" He heard them shouting and laughing like a snarling pack of hyenas chasing after their dinner. "You're dead meat, Teddy boy!"

Teddy didn't know why they always had it out for him. Maybe it was because Brian Belfour's dad had been to jail twice already, and whenever he wasn't in jail, he was dead drunk and always wailing on Brian. Or maybe it was because Jessie Cartwright's mom left Jessie and his younger siblings home alone at night while she went out bar hopping, rolling in at two am every night with someone he knew wasn't his dad. Maybe it was even because Mike Atkins had already been held back twice in school, once in the fourth grade and then again in seventh, and he would probably end of dropping out by the time he reached ninth grade because he still didn't know how to write his name on a paper.

Except Teddy didn't know those things. All Teddy knew was that the Belfour Three had a reputation for causing trouble that was longer than the line down at the community pool during the first week of summer. That, Teddy knew for certain. The other thing Teddy knew was that they had made beating him up their new favorite hobby since the start of the summer, and they really enjoyed it.

And he had made the mistake of forgetting.

"We're coming for you, Teddy," came a quickly approaching voice from behind, followed by a fit of laughter, reminding him that they were still back there, still getting closer. Teddy zigzagged around a kid playing hopscotch on her driveway and then swerved to miss a man walking his dog.

The first time they'd beaten him up had been during the second week of June. School had only been out six days and Teddy had gone down to the library to check out a couple of books to read over summer break. Unfortunately, they caught him while he was riding his bike home, cornering him behind the Blockbuster video store on the corner of Main Street and

Mt. Vernon. When he screamed out for help, they only laughed. Then the punches began.

He had probably ridden his bike by that store a hundred times. One of Teddy's favorite things in the world had been when his mom would take him to the Blockbuster to check out movies and get snacks. But now, anytime he went by the video store, the only memory he had was of the first time he got jumped.

One of the tire rims on his bicycle had twisted that day when he rode it straight into a wall trying to get away. He'd had to walk his bike home the remaining two miles with a bloody nose and a swollen black eye. And to make things even worse, they had ripped up one of the library books like confetti, so he ended up having to do extra chores around the house and even mow a couple lawns so that he could earn money to pay off the book damage fees. The worse part was that Ms. Sanderson, the librarian, even restricted his library card so he wasn't able to check out books the rest of the summer. For Teddy, who devoured books by the day, having his library card restricted was about the equivalent of a death sentence.

"Dude, watch out!" Teddy yelled as he swerved his handlebars again.

"Hey! Watch it, kid!" shouted a heavyset man, washing his car. The man tripped over his bucket of soapy water as Teddy blurred past, spilling water everywhere. Teddy heard something loud bang behind him. He turned to see Mike Atkins, the heaviest of the Belfour Three, lying in a mangled mess. Teddy could hear the heavyset man yelling and cursing.

"You'll pay for that," shouted Brian Belfour, as if Teddy had been the reason for Mike Atkins' soapy collision. "We're going to kill you for that!"

The second time Teddy had been beaten up that summer, he had just walked out of the corner store with a cherry slushy in hand. He just so happened to run straight into them as he was coming out the door. He not only lost the two dollars and fifty cents it cost to buy the slushy when it squished into one of them and then splattered onto the floor, but he had also lost a front tooth after one of them belted him in the mouth.

He'd tried to run that time too, and he would have gotten away if he hadn't have tripped on one of his shoelaces and gone sprawling onto the hard concrete. He'd gotten road rash up both forearms when he braced himself in the fall. That time, he only had to walk a mile home before old Mrs. Peterson picked him up along the way. She lived down the street from Teddy, and he had mowed her lawn a couple of times for five dollars.

"Why's your shirt all red?" Mrs. Peterson had asked, examining him from behind a pair of large, thick glasses that Teddy thought made her eyes look too large for her face.

"I dropped my slushy," Teddy responded solemnly, except "slushy" had come out as "swushy" because of the missing front tooth.

"You know, money doesn't just grow on trees," Mrs. Peterson had said then, as if she was bestowing valuable knowledge on Teddy. "You really should be more careful."

"Ok," Teddy said, nodding out the window. He started thinking about his missing tooth and the wise words spoken from the wrinkly old soothsayer in the seat beside him.

Naturally, Teddy did what any kid in his situation would have done. He locked himself inside his room and played videogames.

After a couple weeks had gone by and with the new school year quickly approaching on the horizon, Teddy had already beaten every videogame he owned, read every book in the house, and reorganized his baseball cards. By that point, he was starting to get bored. Summer had always been his favorite time of the year, but he had almost missed the whole thing, all because he was locked inside of his house like a prisoner.

Teddy had been extra careful not to go outdoors. Not once had he gone down to the community pool, even for the Fourth of July celebration where they sold hot dogs for fifty cents and had both a cotton candy and popcorn machine. If a friend called to see if Teddy wanted to come over, he pretended he was sick or that he had to do chores around the house. If his father told him to go outside and play, he went in the backyard until the coast was clear and then snuck back inside like a common burglar. He even went as far as paying Judy, the little girl next door, to pull out the trashcans for him, something he would soon not be able to afford anymore, since he had stopped mowing lawns around the neighborhood.

Teddy had wanted to take his bike out on several occasions; as it got hotter and hotter, he would often sit in the garage, daydreaming about riding his bike down to the Thrifty's Drugstore to get a scoop of mint and chip or dream about riding over to the ravine behind his house to skip rocks. He'd even been close a few times, but then he would remember the Belfour Three pummeling him into the dirt and knocking out his other front tooth. These moments, all dreams of riding faded away like the quickly passing weeks of Teddy's summer vacation.

He would stand at the edge of the garage, sometimes even sitting on his bike gripping the handlebars, watching the days drift passed, missing out on the magic of summer where stories are made, becoming tomorrow's fond memories that are told for years and years on end, stories he would never be able to tell, staring out at the cracked, black street like a dried up river of hopes and dreams, wishing to travel upon it once again, exploring new frontiers of childhood taking him across an unexplored land, but instead those dreams had been chewed up and spit out like chunks of broken asphalt across the road.

But then his father had killed himself and he had forgotten all about them.

"We're going to turn you into roadkill!" Brian and Jessie were still behind him. When he glanced over his shoulder, Teddy could see that Mike was back in the chase, as well.

"Roadkill!" repeated Jessie. He began to laugh, but Teddy thought Jessie sounded winded, and as Teddy glanced over his shoulder, he saw that Jessie did look like he was starting to fall back to where Mike was.

If he was lucky, maybe they would get tired and just leave him alone. Maybe there's still hope. But then he saw the look on Brian's face. It was one Teddy had seen before, and he knew that it meant death.

Teddy raced down around the corner, his heart feeling like it would burst at any second, praying that he would make it home.

He wondered why he hadn't just stayed inside and why he decided that today would be a good day for a bike ride. Thoughts whipped by like the passing cars on the street.

As Teddy turned another corner, his wheel wobbled, and he almost went toppling over the handlebars, but he was able to maintain his balance. He could hear them on the other street. By some dumb luck, he managed to get even further ahead.

He turned and rode toward the Grand View Bowl, memories flooding passed him of the various theater performances his family had seen there every summer ever since he was five years old. They would dress up in fancy clothes, play clothes, his mother had called them, but not for playing in, she would always remind him. Shakespeare's *Romeo and Juliet* and *A Midsummer's Night Dream* had been just a few of his favorites. Now he felt like he was trapped inside of a nightmare as he rode down the concrete stairs like he was traversing into the trenches of hell with the devil himself riding after him, chasing his long shadow as it stretched down the stairs before him and up the other side as if leading him down a hidden path of salvation that only he could see, a desolate soul climbing the stairway to an unattainable heaven.

"Hey, knucklehead! Over here!" came a voice from up the street. Teddy could see someone waving and shouting up ahead. He peddled even harder. "Hurry! Before they see you!"

Dust went trailing out behind him as Teddy turned onto the dirt road. He all but fell off his bike, exhausted. He began to cough. The other kid, who Teddy had never seen at Grand View Elementary before, grabbed the handlebars and began to run Teddy's bike up the rest of the path toward an old Victorian-style house.

"Come on! Hurry!" The kid disappeared into an small, detached garage, alongside the old house. Teddy followed, slowly getting his breath back. "We'll be safe in here."

"Thanks…a…lot," Teddy said between each gasp of air. They crouched themselves down behind an old rusty Lincoln with the paint peeling off in patches. The car made Teddy think of the big dalmatian dog that lived at the house from down the street. Teddy looked around. There were a bunch of old tools hanging from the walls, cobwebs everywhere. "I'm pretty sure you just saved my life."

"Don't mention it. There were kids like that where I used to live. Name's David. David Gonzalez."

The kid stuck his hand out, and Teddy shook it.

"I'm Teddy Stafford. You're new in town? I don't remember seeing you at school before."

"You got it. Me and my folks just moved in," David said, grinning as he stood up and walked toward the opening of the garage. "I think we're safe now. I don't hear them anymore."

Teddy got up and followed. He thought it was funny, the way David called his parents, folks.

"Your parents just moved you here?" Teddy questioned as he looked at the old house that reminded him of a larger version of the creepy dollhouse he had seen his neighbor Judy playing with in the front yard of her house. He knew that David had just saved him, and he didn't want to be rude, but he thought that this house didn't look safe. In fact, it looked like a place that bums or druggies would hang out in. Shingles were hanging from the roof haphazardly, and Teddy thought the windows resembled sleepy eyes, the way that a few of the shutters were dangling in front of them, threatening to fall off any second. There were two missing steps leading up to the porch like broken teeth, where an old swing was dangling from one rusty chain, squeaking in the breeze. Teddy could tell that the house had been green at one point, but the paint was chipping, and the house mostly looked brown and sad now. Even the grass and bushes in front of the house looked tired and overgrown, like a tangled net trying to conceal something inside.

"And what's that supposed to mean?" David asked, crossing his arms defensively across his chest.

"It's just that, I never even knew this place was up here until today," Teddy said, rubbing his hair nervously as he began to stammer. "It just doesn't look like a place someone would move into."

"If that's your way of saying thanks for saving your life," David said, eyes narrowing, "then I guess, you're welcome."

"Ah, man, I'm sorry. I didn't mean it like that," Teddy said as his face started to look like he had been out in the sun too long.

David stared at Teddy for a moment, and then his eyes widened and he began to laugh hysterically.

"You crack me up," David said, slapping Teddy on the back playfully. "I'm just busting your chops. My folks are renovating the place. Midlife crisis. Some people buy a new sports car or go on a really expensive vacation, but my folks, they buy an old house to fix up. Jeepers! I wish you could have seen your face."

"Okay, okay, you got me," said Teddy, starting to laugh, as well. He examined the kid in front of him, as if really seeing him now for the first time, now that they were safe. David was wearing a checkered button-down shirt with blue slacks and brown slip-on shoes. Teddy thought David looked like he had just come from church, except it wasn't Sunday, especially since David's short black hair was neatly parted to the side, as well. "Dude, you really had me going. Where are you from anyways?"

"We're originally from down south," David answered. Teddy guessed that explained David's funny slang and fancy clothes. "How old are you?"

"Twelve. How about you?"

"Same. Come on, I'll show you around."

Renovating. It made sense. But still, as Teddy followed David down the dirt path around the back side of the house, he couldn't help but think that the place still didn't look like someone had just moved in. If he was honest, this place looked like it was going to take a very long time before it even began to look at least half way habitable.

David led Teddy to the back of the house. They made their way through an old wooden gate with a few planks missing. The backyard looked just as bad as the front, maybe even worse. There were overgrown plants everywhere, and Teddy was almost sure he saw something scurry into the tall grass as he and David entered its domain like two foreign intruders. He felt they were Lewis and Clark exploring uncharted territory, and he couldn't help but wonder when was the last time that someone had been back there.

"Oh! What is that smell?" Teddy plugged his nose. "It smells like something died back here."

"Come over here, and I'll show you." David pushed through some of the tall grass and Teddy followed hesitantly. "Look."

Teddy hadn't even seen it when he first entered the backyard because the tall grass had obscured it from view. Hidden in the center of the backyard was an old in-ground swimming pool that now looked like a pond. The water was murky green and Teddy saw that there were even some plants growing in the pool that he thought might be lily pads like the ones he had seen down at the lake.

"I'm pretty sure that there's something dead in there," Teddy said as he swatted at some flies that were buzzing near the pool.

"I'm pretty sure you're right. Dad says he's going to fix it up and that hopefully I can have a pool party by the end of summer, which is only about five weeks away."

"That would be awesome," Teddy replied, but he didn't think David would be having any pool parties this summer, or, even the next. In fact, he was pretty sure it would take a couple of years before the smell was gone.

"Check this out."

Teddy hadn't even realized that David had left his side because he was too busy looking at the pool. Something was bubbling in the pool water, and he wondered what was under the surface. He turned to see David standing at the far end of the yard in front of an oak tree that towered over the house. The backyard had seemed a little dark when they first walked in, but Teddy had just assumed it was the shadow from the house. But now, standing beside David in front of the oak tree, Teddy could see that it was the tree and not the house, that was shading the yard, making it feel gloomy and cold, even though it was a bright, hot day in July, and it wasn't even close to noon yet.

Both boys stood there, side by side, each knowing how lucky they were, for every boy dreams of having a tree like this in his backyard.

"You want to help me build a treehouse?" David asked, turning toward Teddy and smiling his big toothy grin again.

Teddy looked up at the large oak, and his imagination began to go wild. He had always dreamed of building a treehouse like in *The Swiss Family Robinson* or even a fortress like in *Robinson Crusoe*, but he didn't have any trees big enough in his yard. That, and he knew his mom would have an aneurism if he was climbing a tree as big as this. But his mom didn't need to know about this. If his father was able to keep his secrets, Teddy felt that he could keep this one just fine himself.

"You bet I do," Teddy replied, throwing his arm over David's shoulder.

"Swell," said David. "Well then, let's get started."

Beneath the old oak tree, weather worn and strained, standing longer than time could tell, minds racing, contemplating endless possibilities. Their tree now. Perhaps growing for a millennia just for them and this moment. Contrived dreams of boys with half a summer still ahead, orchestrated by nature herself.

Deep roots.

Clinging to dirt and secrets spilled.

PART TWO

BENEATH THE SUN AND STARS

CHAPTER 4

They worked on the treehouse all week, from sunup to sundown. Teddy woke every morning before the sun came up and packed two sack lunches for him and David with peanut butter and jelly sandwiches, apples, and a couple fruit punch Capri Suns. His mom never asked what he was doing. She was just happy to see that Teddy was going outside again, something she was beginning to wonder if he would ever do again.

To build the treehouse, the boys used the old tools that were hanging in the garage. A few were rusted, but most were surprisingly still in good condition. David was able to find a big box of contractor nails, too. The box looked like it was from the 40s' or 50s', but the nails were still shiny. There were even a bunch of wood planks piled up behind the garage that they were able to use to build the structure of the treehouse. First, though, they had to kill about a dozen black widows and chase off a 'possum that had been using the wood as a home.

They had become fast friends, the two boys who had never known of the other's existence at summer's start. There is a special bond that is formed between boys during the summertime, a unique connection stretching across a millennia, traversing back to the dawn of time, extending perhaps even passed. Give two boys a couple of hammers and bucketful of nails and something to build together and they become friends for life by summer's end. Sooner, if they're lucky.

"I was thinking," said David as he wiped his arm across his forehead and then hammered another nail into a board.

"You sure that's wise?" asked Teddy as he climbed up the plank ladder they nailed into the tree. "You might end up hurting yourself."

"Okay, wise guy. Laugh it up." David finished hammering the board he was holding and stood back to look at his progress. "I was thinking that this place should be done in a day or two and that maybe we could take a break."

Teddy looked around at their hideout. It was no *Swiss Family Robinson* treehouse that he had imagined in his mind, that was for sure, but in his humble opinion, it was pretty close. They had already made the deck of the treehouse and had built three of the four walls. Work was coming along nicely, and David was right. If they kept working at their pace, they would be done in two or three days, max.

"Okay. What did you have in mind?"

"I'm glad you asked, Teddy, my boy. You see that orange grove over there? The one at the foot of that hill?

Teddy looked through the window of the treehouse and nodded. He had never really noticed it before, but he saw that there was in fact an orange grove that stretched for at least a mile behind David's house.

"Right," continued David. "So, I've been itching to go exploring ever since we moved here, and I was thinking that those orange groves would be great for lizard hunting."

"Lizard hunting?" Teddy said, raising one eyebrow.

"Don't tell me you've never been lizard hunting?"

"No, never."

"Oh, boy, are you in for a treat! We used to go lizard hunting all the time back at my old place. I actually hold the record for most lizards caught in a day." David tilted his head proudly and smiled as he made this statement, as if this was an amazing accomplishment that Teddy should know all about. "Thirty-seven. I'm pretty sure that record will stand for at least a hundred years. Maybe even more."

David looked at Teddy matter-of-factly while Teddy looked at David like he was crazy.

"What do you do with them? I mean, after you catch them?"

"Why, you eat them of course. You poke them onto a stick like a skewer and then roast them over a fire. Best thing in the whole world."

"Dude, that's nasty."

Teddy looked like he was about to be sick.

David laughed.

"I'm just yanking your chain. Don't go hurling all over the place. Of course you don't eat them. You just let the little guys go back into the wild."

"What's the point then?"

David's jaw nearly hit the ground. He stared at Teddy, dumbfounded.

"What's the point? The point, is that it's fun. That's the point. Come on, I'll show you. All we need is a couple buckets. I'm pretty sure I saw a few in the garage."

They had been working hard all week, and Teddy thought that a break did sound nice. Plus, Teddy thought he could beat David's record. He set his hammer down on the floor of the almost-finished treehouse, flipped his ballcap around, and then followed David down the ladder and into the garage.

David had been right about the buckets, handing Teddy a cracked bucket with some dried dirt caked to the sides. Teddy was pretty sure that the buckets had probably been used for plants, maybe even some of the ones that were now overtaking the yard. Whoever had lived here before had all sorts of things stored away in the garage. Not only was there the big old Lincoln and all the tools they had been using to build the treehouse, but there were stacks of old magazines piled atop a desk that looked like it probably weighed a ton, several boxes piled against one side of the garage, and even an old ham radio.

Teddy guessed that the guy who used to live here had died, and that was why all of his old junk had been left behind.

Taking a break to explore the orange groves had been a great idea. There were at least a hundred rows of orange trees, and each had more than twenty trees. Teddy didn't think he had ever seen so many trees in his life. The two boys walked side by side up and down each row, in search of unsuspecting lizards to add to their buckets. The trees cast thick shadows making Teddy feel like Bilbo Baggins exploring Mirkwood Forrest.

David had been right again. Lizard hunting was a lot of fun. Teddy was catching on quickly, but he had a good teacher. David told Teddy that the key to catching lizards was patience. He showed Teddy that in order to catch a lizard, you needed to sneak up by crouching down quietly, moving your hand out slowly, and then quickly grabbing the lizard by the tail. And David wasn't just good at lizard hunting, he was great. For every lizard Teddy caught, David caught double. But still, Teddy was having more fun than he had in a while.

"There's one right there."

He was good at seeing them, but he gave Teddy first try with nearly all of them.

"I see it."

"Just creep up slow, like I showed you."

"Alright, thanks."

Teddy crept slowly to where David had pointed on the tree, his eyes not moving from the lizard. He jumped, reaching his hand out quickly, but tripped and fell over a root and instead sprawling flat on his face, squishing a few oranges that were lying about on the ground.

"Great, it got away."

"You were really close that time though. You're doing really good."

"You don't have to lie. You're way better at this."

Teddy pushed himself off the floor and rubbed his hands down the front of his jeans.

"Don't beat yourself up. You almost had that one. It just takes practice, that's all."

"Maybe, but I think if we were to spend every day out here this summer, I still wouldn't be as good as you. Where'd you learn to catch lizards anyways?"

"My dad taught me and he says that my granddaddy taught him before that."

"That's really cool. My father used to teach me—" Teddy stopped.

David looked at him, but didn't say anything.

The boys continued to walk through the rows of orange trees. Both were quiet for a while, neither speaking a word. Just walking and listening to the sounds of the grove. They walked down long rows, up and down, not going anywhere in particular but to where the dirt path led them. They stepped over dry leaves and decomposing oranges that had fallen from the trees, a frosted white powder wafting over the ground whenever either of them was unfortunate enough to trample one of the abandoned fruits, the smell sickeningly sweet. Several quail ran across the trails, hiding between the tress and the shrubbery beneath.

"My father's dead," Teddy said, breaking the silence. "He—"
Teddy paused again and then stopped walking.

David looked at him, nodding his head slowly. He walked over to Teddy, who had his head down, and then put his arm around Teddy's shoulder. "You don't need to say anything."

They spent the remainder of the day walking through the orange groves as the sun moved over head, mapping the progress of the day. It was warm, but under the trees it felt almost cool, especially when a breeze would roll through the branches making the leaves shutter like hundreds of old windchimes each merging together to create a melodic symphony whose only audience was the two boys passing beneath the branches. Every so often they would hear a crow crying out, sending a warning to the other birds that two intruders were wandering through the grove, and then the boys would see a murder of crows flutter into the distance as they crept through the trees, gnarled branches, some like arthritic fingers, the birds cawing angrily as the boys passed underneath their resting place, weaving a trail across uncharted territory.

As the day moved forward, the boys guiding the sun, leading it across the grey blue sky, they came upon a concrete wash where the runoff from heavy summer rainstorms would at times come down the hills that stood behind the orange groves, occasionally creating a river that would then flow beneath the city, but for now, the wash was dry. A chain-link fence ran the length of the dried up concrete stream and the boys walked along the barrier looking for an opening that they could pass through to reach the ravine down below. Red and yellow signs hung on the fence, warning of danger and the consequences that would befall those who trespassed, but to boys on the cusp of quickly approaching teenage years, the metal signs were merely calls to an awaiting adventure. A challenge pointing them in the direction of something far better, awaiting them in the shadows of the high walls of the gorge down below. They were pioneers like Daniel Boone and Davy Crockett, but instead of a vast forest of unexplored terrain with violent rivers cutting paths across the land, the boys had the groves and the concrete canyon, and to them, they were just as much frontiersmen as any who had traveled the land before them, and any who would come after.

"You see that?"

"What?" Teddy looked where David was pointing.

"Over there. There's an opening in the fence."

"I see it. Good eye."

"Thanks. Here I'll hold the fence and you climb through."

David grabbed onto the part of the fence where someone had cut an opening, and pulled the two sides apart. Teddy passed through the opening, and then once on the other side, he held the fence apart, returning the favor for David.

"We'll have to drop down."

"I don't know. It looks pretty far." Teddy peeked over the edge, surveying the rocky terrain below.

"There's nowhere to climb and those walls are too steep."

"We can always walk down toward the hills."

"There's no other way," David said, looking into the gorge.

"There's got to be a lower place."

"Yeah, but that will take too long. Here, I'll lower you down."

David laid down on his stomach on the ridge of the concrete cavern and held out his hands. Teddy grabbed them and then climbed down the wall like an excavator traversing into an underground cave. Once he was far enough down, he let go of David's hands and then dropped to the floor, his shoes crunching the sand and gravel that had settled in the ravine.

"Alright, your turn. It's not too far down. Just hang and I'll catch you."

"Okay, but you better not let me fall."

"Hey, I trusted you, so know it's your turn to trust me."

David lowered himself down the side of the concrete wall and then dropped. Teddy caught him, but the weight of the other boy made him fall, and the two boys crumbled like a sack of dirty laundry.

"I thought you were going to catch me," David said.

"I did, didn't I."

"If that's what you call catching, I'd hate to see you play ball."

"Well, it's not my fault your scrawny ass is heavier than it looks."

The two boys laughed, brushing off their pants, and then looked around the urban creek that had long since dried up. Scrubby tufts of weeds pushed up through the cracks in the cement and several large rocks lay scattered about. Empty beer cans, aluminum, rusted with the labels sun washed and faded, were strewn about haphazardly. Graffiti clung to walls, ancient markings scrawled in indecipherable script. Shards of green and brown glass, jagged remnants broken and forgotten. Pirate's lost treasure. Overhead, a hawk circled, crying out loud screeches across the valley as it hovered over the brown rolling hills that sat behind the orange groves. The two boys walked the length of the wash, sun beating on their heads, until they came upon a large concrete tunnel at the end of the ravine. They paused for another moment and Teddy pulled out the hanky he had been carrying in his back pocket and then wiped the sweat from his brow. He passed it to David and he did the same, then he handed it back to Teddy. A metal grate of twisted rebar steel covered the entrance to the storm drain. If they were to go any further today, they would need tools to pry the rebar open, in order to access the tunnel and what lied beyond. They had reached the end of the trail and the end of the orange grove, going further than either of them had ever gone before. They stood there, an understanding passing between the two of them, enjoying the moment that they would forever share, then they turned around, walking back along the ravine and heading the way they had come.

They walked back through the orange grove. The sun was falling in the west, red streaks creased the sky. The shadows under the trees were quickly vanishing and instead, a dull fading grey light was taking their place like someone was pulling a dark sheet, covering the trees.

As they followed the dark rows of trees back toward home, Teddy felt his foot sink into something squishy. "Oh, dude! Gross!"

"Jeepers! There's maggots all over it."

Teddy lifted his foot from off the dead cat. A few of the maggots had crawled onto his shoe and were making their way toward Teddy's laces.

"Ah! Nasty!" Teddy shook his foot and maggots flung into the dirt. David started laughing, and Teddy began to jump up and down. "Not cool, dude. Not cool."

"Sorry, it's just that, I didn't know you could jitter bug so good. You were dancing like your feet were on fire."

"Whatever. You'd do the same too, if it was you." Teddy shook his foot some more and then began to swing his arms back in forth, snapping his fingers. David, still laughing, began to do the same.

"What do you think killed it?" asked Teddy, inching back toward the dead cat to get a better look.

"I don't know. Could have been a snake or maybe even a hawk. I did see one flying around earlier." David paused, looking down at the dead cat. The trees rustled above.

"We should probably bury it."

"Bury it? Why?"

"Because it was someone's pet," Teddy said solemnly. He pointed to the collar around the tabby cat's neck. "Someone loved it and it deserves to be buried."

David looked from the cat to Teddy. He was used to seeing Teddy laughing and smiling, but he was pretty sure that he could see tears in Teddy's eyes. "Okay, we'll bury it."

They walked back to David's house, counting the trees along the way, so they wouldn't forget where the cat was. David found a couple shovels in the garage and Teddy found a black marker and some rope in one of the drawers of the metal desk. Then he grabbed two planks of wood from the pile behind the garage.

"For the grave marker," Teddy said, when he saw David looking at him.

The two boys walked side by side in silence, counting trees along the way, back to the dead cat. They dug the hole together, piling the dirt into a little mound next to it, and then Teddy used his shovel to lift the cat inside. While David filled in the hole, Teddy wrote out the grave marker. When they were finished, both boys pushed the makeshift headstone into the soft dirt at the head of the grave, and then they walked back to David's house.

On the grave marker, Teddy wrote:

The BEST Cat Anyone Could Ask For.
He Was Loved.

CHAPTER 5

When they got to the top of Oak Street, Teddy and David jumped off their bikes and wheeled them the rest of the way. They pushed their bikes off the concrete sidewalk and onto the dirt path they had been riding toward that morning, bypassing the metal access bar blocking the entrance of the pathway, going around it instead. Once around, they hoped back onto their bikes and began the trek up one of the several trails leading up Azure Mountain, a hill really more than it was a mountain, but to them, the name didn't matter.

Sitting behind several of the wood streets making up a prominent portion of Grand View's suburban housing developments, the rolling mountain stretched across the eastern horizon, where it rose up, round peek meeting the blue skies behind. At the morning's dawn, the sun would climb up and over the backside of the hill, casting a long shadow out over the city, the brilliant light colliding with the sky to create the illusion of a blue hill rising above the city. Like a watchful abuela. Skin wrinkled and harsh. Wrapping her arms around the city, under her protective gaze.

The boys rode their bikes through the backcountry over rolling hills. Waves in a desert. They were the ships upon warm rough water. Shrubs poking up all around. Brambles and thickets threatening to poke holes in their tires as they rode across terrain neither had ever explored before. Harsh thickets and spreading cactus hiding quail, scurrying across the path as the boys pressed forward without a care in the world, for theirs was only the day ahead and the adventure that awaited them beyond the mountains.

A lone roadrunner guarding the path, watched as they approached, a headdress of feathers standing tall like a proud native chief from a rival tribe. The boys were whooping Indians upon the backs of fierce steeds. Stampeding across the hills on metal horses. Shouting a war cry echoing death to all daring to challenge.

Burros wandered in the distance. Brought to the hills of the Inland Empire in the 1840s and 50s by miners. Prospectors looking to make a fortune from unclaimed gold hiding within the caves and mountains of California, then domesticated in the 1950s by rancheros looking to start a new life in a new valley. Pack animals used to cart tools and equipment, now wandering free. Roaming across the rocky landscape. Permanent fixtures like the hills they now meandered through. As much a part of the mountain as the dirt beneath their dusty hooves.

"This ought to be fun."

"What?'

"Over there." David pointed.

"What? I just see more hills."

"Exactly. Come on."

"Come on where?"

"Just come on, would you?"

They rode their bikes a little ways off the trail and came across several small hills, bumps carved into the soil by nature, or perhaps by fellow travelers before them. A makeshift racetrack waiting to be ridden. Hardened and preserved by the beating sun. After a further look, they came to the conclusion that someone had spent several hours perfecting a haven for riders looking to enjoy a challenge. A place where boys could be boys without the fear of a watchful eye warning them otherwise. A place of broken bones. Scrapes and blood. Fighting and cursing. A crevice of land cut into the hillside where boys could become men and those who couldn't could ride back down the mountain back home.

"See, I told you."

"This place is really cool. You sure we won't get in trouble?"

"In trouble? Why would we get in trouble?"

"I don't know. What if the kids who made it come back?" An unease settled on Teddy. He glanced around, shuddering, even though there was no breeze and the sun was already set high up above.

"You're worried that the Belfour Three made this, aren't you?"

"I mean, yeah. Aren't you?"

"The way I figure is, this is free country. Wild country where anything goes."

"That's exactly what I am afraid of. If anything goes, well that means if they catch us up here then there is no one up here to stop them."

"If them boys made it, well then they are going to have to catch us first, and last I remember was they didn't catch you the last time. Besides, this is our country. We own these hills, not them."

Teddy looked at David and shook his head. "How do you do that?"

"Do what?"

"Not care."

"Oh shit, I care about a lot of things. I just don't care much for bullies telling me what I can and can't do. Like I said, this is free country. Wild country. You and I have just as much every right to be up here as the Belfour Three do. Or anyone else for that matter."

Teddy began to nod. He realized in that moment that David was like no kid he had met before. And he also realized that David was right.

"Alright then. Well in that case, try to keep up."

"Nah. You try to keep up. Eat my dust!"

They raced their bikes off the path, riding down onto the dirt track, the sun moving from the eastern hemisphere into the western hemisphere across the vivid blue sky. They rode the track, racing not only each other, but time itself.

They came upon an open area on the hillside. The mountain rose up steep before them. A retaining wall made of cinder blocks obstructed the pathway. The only way from here was back down or climb over the wall.

They left their bikes, hiding them behind some bushes and began to climb. Once they reached the top they continued on their way, except the path was gone. Thickets and tumbleweeds grew haphazardly across the hillside. Rocks cast shadows as large as houses. The boys climbed over some and others they were able to merely go around. Wild rabbits sat chewing on yellow sun-scorched grass, noses twitching beneath watchful eyes as the boys walked passed.

"Do you hear that?"

"Yeah, I hear it. It's a rattler."

"A rattlesnake?" Teddy slowed his pace, looking down the unmarked path they were forging.

"Yeah. And from the sound of it, it's close by."

"Great," Teddy said.

"Don't worry. Snakes are afraid of people. As long as you don't startle it or make it feel threatened, you'll be fine."

"I'll make sure to remember that."

"Or it could be a Chupacabra." David looked at Teddy, eyes like saucers. He stopped walking and Teddy did as well.

"Chupa what?"

"Chupacabras. My dad told me they are known to roam these hills."

"I've never hear of a Chupacabra before. What is it?"

"They're sort of like half wild dog, half lizard, but usually they only come out at night, so I think we're safe. But that rattle sure did sound like it could be one."

"You're making that up. No way is there a half dog, half lizard. That's not genetically possible."

"Oh its possible. When the cowboys were spreading across the land and they started making ranches and would run their cattle all over these valleys, they started reporting that their cattle would sometimes be found dead in the morning. Blood sucked out of them. Dry as a toothpick."

"That has got to be the craziest story I've ever heard. And I've read a lot of books. You're full of shit."

"No, it's true. Eventually, as these lands became more civilized the Chupacabras were forced into the hills, just like the burros and the rabbits you see up here. And like I said, they only come out at night, so that's why you've probably never seen one before."

"Well if they are real, how do they survive up here then? What do they eat?"

"I think they mostly eat the rabbits, but dad says they have been known to eat the wild donkeys too, on occasion."

Teddy looked at the sky. It was turning red. The sun was closer now to the ground than it was to the sky when they had started. "Do you think maybe we should head back?"

"No, I'm sure we'll be fine. Unless."

"Unless what?"

"Unless the sun goes down. Maybe we should head back to our bikes."

"I think so too. Come on."

As they headed back down the hill, David crouched down and picked up a rock, tossing it off into the bushes.

"What was that?" Teddy stammered, looking the direction David had thrown the rock.

The sun was now setting even further and a few stars could be seen.

"Teddy. Don't move."

"What? Why?"

"I think I see something. Out there in the bushes." He knelt down and Teddy did the same. "Don't you see it?

"No. I don't see anything. Come on. Let's go."

"Don't move. It'll see you. Be still."

"Oh shit! I do see it. There. In the bushes."

Teddy looked at David and grabbed his shoulder.

"I think it sees us. Here it comes. We got to run."

Teddy got up and ran. Something crashed through the thickets behind him. He almost stumbled but kept his balance, then stopped. He could hear David laughing from behind him. Standing about ten feet away from him was a burro. It looked at the boys then trotted off to find its family.

"Real funny. Laugh it up."

"You should have seen your face. Classic."

"How long did you know it was a burro for?"

"Pretty much the whole time. I saw it when we were walking passed that big boulder over there. I bet you thought you were about to get your blood sucked from the Chupacabra."

David laughed even harder, falling onto the ground.

"Are there even really such things as Chupacabras?" Teddy asked.

"I mean, yeah. In Mexican legends and stuff."

"I'm not going to lie. You got me."

Teddy began to laugh too.

David rolled around even more, laughing. Tears were rolling down his cheeks. "Oh, shit! Something bit me."

"Sure, dude. I'm not falling for any more of your pranks."

"No, I'm serious. Something bit my ass. I think a real rattler got me."

"The only ass I see is you and that burro that just ran off into the hills."

"You have to suck the venom out Teddy or I'm done for. It really hurts." David had stopped laughing and was now standing and rubbing his bottom.

"Are you serious?"

"Dead serious in a minute if you don't get this venom out of me."

Teddy watched David's face turned as white as the moon, rising in the sky above them.

"Looks like you're a goner then because there is no way in hell I'm sucking venom from your ass. I'll make sure to tell your parents you loved them."

"Come on Teddy. I thought we were friends." Real panic was in David' voice now.

"Okay, okay. Calm down. Look to your left."

"To my left? What? Why"

"Just look."

David grew quiet, then began nodding his head. "How long did you know for?"

"Pretty much right when you fell down and began rolling around. I wanted to warn you but you looked like you were having too much fun at my expense."

David stared at the ground and began to laugh. Teddy was laughing too. A bramble of disturbed cactus was growing near his feet.

They pedaled off the trail, riding home under faint moonlight. The streetlights were starting to come on. Beacons in the night, signals for them that it was time to return home. They rode their bikes down the sidewalk and then onto the street. A brown owl flew overhead, then landed within a large sycamore tree. Passing cars began to switch on their headlights, beams like glowing trails cut into the darkness.

David cut across Main Street and Teddy followed. Store signs slowly became illuminated and downtown Grand View flickered to life. A couple crossed the street ahead of the boys, going into a coffeeshop and a few families were coming out of the diner. The boys passed a group of college students walking along the sidewalk. They were laughing and then entered a tavern. Strings of lights hung overhead, strewn from one side of the road to the other like fallen stars over the street.

They rode their bikes through the quiet shadows of Grant Park. Grey specters briefly passing through time changing before their eyes. Wisps of air, fleeting breaths hovering upon the twilight sky, flickering candles burning for a fixed moment within the darkness of the approaching end of day.

They could hear the sprinklers click on in the distance. Teddy watched as David suddenly veered across the grass, heading straight toward the stream of water, and then he followed. His wheels sprayed water out behind him. He could hear him, up ahead, riding his bike through the water like rain falling. Laughter booming like thunder. Teddy was laughing too.

David looked over his shoulder and then turned his bike, riding back toward Teddy. They rode in circles, crisscrossing across the wet summer grass. He grinned his big toothy smile, watching as Teddy threw his hands up over his head like a bird flying in the nighttime sky. He thrust his hands over his head as well, and both boys rode through the grass as if they were soaring in the grey ashen clouds above. Teddy's cheeks glistened in the moonlight, and David couldn't tell if it was water from the sprinklers that was running down his friend's cheeks or if it was tears and soon realized it was both, for he could hear Teddy sobbing.

They dropped their bikes and stripped off their shirts, running beneath the stars and among them. Crying out into the night. Screaming to be heard. Listening for a reply that did not come. They were the last two people in the world.

They laid down, feeling the prickle of the grass on their bare skin. Teddy knew he'd regret it later because he was going to have one hell of an itch on his back in the morning, and maybe even a rash, but right now, he couldn't care less.

"I'm sorry."

"About what?"

"About your father. I'm sorry he died."

Teddy was quiet for a moment. Thinking. "Me too."

The boys stared up at the sky, hands resting behind their heads.

"Do you think there's a heaven?"

"I think so. Don't you?" Teddy asked, turning and looking at David.

"Maybe. But what if there's not?"

"Well, I mean, people have to go somewhere when they die, right?"

"Yeah, I guess so. But what if they don't?"

"Don't what?'

It was David who had now become quiet. He sighed deeply. "Don't go to heaven."

"Well I guess they go to the other place then."

"You mean hell."

"Yeah. That's what I learned in Sunday school from the teacher, at least."

"But what if a person doesn't go to either place?"

"Well I guess that would make them a ghost then."

"Do you believe in ghosts?"

"Not any more than I believe in heaven and hell I guess."

"I couldn't imagine playing a harp on a cloud for the rest of my life, and I definitely couldn't imagine burning in a lake of fire for all eternity either."

"Me either."

"I couldn't imagine being a ghost either. What about kids?"

"What about them?"

"Do you think they go to heaven and hell when they die?"

"Probably just heaven. I can't see why they'd go to hell."

"You're probably right. I guess for them, they only get two options then."

"How so?"

"Up in heaven playing a harp or down here being a ghost. Neither sound great to me."

They laid that way for a while. Around them the trees swayed softly.

Teddy glanced over at David again. He could tell something was bothering him. "Now that I think about it, if there is a God, I think he probably lets us pick," said Teddy.

"Pick? Even the bad people?"

"No, them he sends straight to hell. I think he lets kids pick though."

"What do you mean, pick?"

"I think if a kid dies before their time, then God lets them pick if they want to stay up there with him, playing their harp, or he lets them come back for a little while longer. But not as a ghost."

"As what then?"

"I think he lets them come back as an angel."

"An angel?"

"I think he lets them come back to do one more good deed, that way they feel like they weren't shortchanged. Then, once they've helped, playing a harp probably sounds pretty nice."

"That does sound better than being a ghost."

"I think so too."

"I'm sorry about the Chupacabra."

"That's okay. I'm sorry about the cactus. Does it still hurt?"

"Just a little. I think my jeans got the worst of it."

The two boys laid side by side underneath the blanket of stars like boys were supposed to do, neither knowing that moments like these were becoming rarer with each passing summer day and that in fifty years' time, it would be moments like these that would be remembered and yearned for the most. Under the setting stars of summer, thinking back to when the dog days of summer wept.

CHAPTER 6

He had a dream about him that night. His father. It was the first time since he had died that Teddy had dreamt about him. It was nighttime in the dream too, and his father was in the garage sitting atop the back of a burro. The only light, coming from the lamp atop his father's workbench. He was wearing the same clothes he had been wearing when Teddy had discovered him hanging from the end of the rope. Blue jeans, white t-shirt, and barefoot. His brown work boots with the scuffed toes and dried concrete splotches that he always wore were sitting on the metal shoe rack against the wall. Teddy's mom hated when her husband came home, tracking dirt through the house, especially after she had cleaned the floors, so she always made him take off his boots and keep them in the garage. Before he killed himself, Teddy's father took off his shoes, went inside the house and wrote the letter, and then came back out into the garage.

Even before he killed himself, he had made sure to keep his wife's floors clean.

The mess he left for her and Teddy to clean up afterward was a whole different story.

Teddy walked out into his father's sacred place. His father was staring out the open garage door into the night. Both the burro he was sitting atop and he himself were completely still. Just staring into the darkness. Pitch black like tar. Black abyss threatening to overtake them. Suffocating. The mouth of hell. Around his neck he was wearing the rope he had hung himself with. Noose tied tight like a dress tie, which Teddy had never seen his father wear a minute before in all his years on earth. The rope looked oddly out of place, but at the same time fitting. As if he had always been meant to wear the rope or a tie, and in the end he had decided upon the rope. His final dress clothes that he would wear to the grave and forever after.

He stood beside his father. The burro shifted, hooves clacking against the concrete, and Teddy heard the rope creak from the wooden beam above.

"Why'd you do it?" Teddy looked up at his father.

"Why does anybody do anything?" His father did not look at him. Only continued to stare out into the black nighttime sky.

"That's not an answer."

"Isn't?"

Teddy stood quietly. Contemplating the answer.

"I loved you. Me and mom both did."

"There was never a doubt in my mind about that."

The burro shifted again. It took a step forward. The rope around his father's neck tightened, but his father didn't seem to notice. He looked like a cowboy from one of those old western movies, except he was the bad guy atop the horse about to be hung by the sheriff at high noon for committing a crime punishable by death. His cheeks looked scruffy and his normally short hair looked unkempt. Teddy couldn't tell for sure, it was too dark, but it looked like his father had lost weight, making him look skeletal and frail. Not like the father he remembered who was strong and orderly. Teddy wondered if he was perhaps seeing the real version of his father now. The one no one was able to see before. The father who he kept hidden inside for no one to see.

"But you didn't love us."

"Never say that."

"If you did, then you wouldn't have killed yourself."

"That's the reason why I did it."

"Because you loved us?"

"Yes."

The burro took another step forward again, tightening the cord around his father's neck even more. This time his father grimaced. His teeth looked grey like grimy stones as if he had been chewing on ash, small wisps of smoke escaped from the corners his mouth. The faint scent of sulfur lingered in the garage, escaping from his father like an altar server swinging a thurible of incense during the entrance procession of a church service. Sanctifying his own coffin and place of eternal rest.

"That doesn't make any sense."

"It does to me."

"People don't kill themselves because they love someone."

"They do if it's the best thing for them."

"The best thing for who? You?"

"No. The best thing for you and your mother."

"Killing yourself was the best thing for us?"

"Yes."

"How is that?"

"It was the only way to keep you safe."

Again the burro stepped forward. Teddy knew the next step would probably be the last. Smoke was now billowing from his father's mouth like the exhaust from his old rusted truck. But this, his father couldn't fix. Not this time anyways. It was too late to fix anything anymore. His father was finished fixing things. It was Teddy's turn now to fix things, only he still didn't know how. Either that, or he chose not to.

"But I was safe."

"Not from me you weren't."

"Why not?"

"Because of the itch."

"What itch?"

"The one digging into my mind like a black worm."

Teddy looked at his father and then at the burro. He watched as the animal's muscles tensed and knew his time was up. The burro's tail began to swish back and forth nervously, as if anticipating the next moment. A moment the animal had been waiting for the whole night. Its eyes, full moons eagerly searching for the next moment in time. It was the vessel that would fulfill a destiny that had already been written in the black starry night of eternity, the harbinger of death leading to the gates of hell and beyond. Smoke was now rising from his father's ears and nose, seeping from his pores. The whole garage was a thick, suffocating black fog. The putrid smell of sulfur was overwhelming and Teddy began to cough, then gag, choking on the stale ashes of his dead father.

"Please, don't go."

"I have to."

"Please, just stay a little longer."

"You know I can't do that."

"Please. Stay for me papa. Please, don't leave me again."

His father turned and looked at him. Teddy had called him a name he hadn't called him since he was a small child. His father was now completely covered in smoke. He was weeping ash. "But that's how I save you."

His father slapped the burro's hindside. It reared up slightly on its hindlegs and then ran forward. The rope snapped from the high up wooden beam with a loud crack and Teddy's father and the burro disappeared into the darkness. Only the dead rapping of the burro's hooves could be heard in the black abyss.

It was the thunder that woke Teddy from his dream. He was sitting atop his bike in the garage and the door was open. Outside it was raining and it was still night. The wind howled and a streak of lightening lit up the sky, then blackness again. He crossed his arms over his chest and rubbed his arms. Hanging from the high up wooden beam was the rope his father had hung himself with. The noose dangled above Teddy's head. An invitation to follow.

Teddy gripped the handlebars on his bike. He began to shiver. His hair was matted to his forehead, thick with sweat. Somewhere beyond the garage, he watched as his father rode amongst the night on the back of the wild donkey. Trailing behind him was the frayed rope. The clack of the burro's hooves like thunder.

He slowly pushed his feet up, standing on the bike peddles. Teddy lifted one foot and placed it on the bike's seat. The bike wobbled on the kickstand, but held steady. He lifted his other foot until he had both atop the seat. To someone passing by on the street, Teddy would have looked funny, back arched as he slowly raised himself, standing upon his bike's seat. But no one passed by.

Teddy slowly released one hand from the bike grip. He reached his hand above him until he could feel the coarse rope and then grabbed on. He let go of the other handlebar grip and slowly stood, using the cord to pull himself up so that he was now standing atop his bike. Slowly, he placed the noose around his neck. It scratched against his Adam's apple. He was an acrobat performing for an audience of none.

Only the ghost of his father.

He was watching closely.

Grey teeth grinning against the black of the night.

"Boy, howdy!" David was standing in the opening of the garage. The rain streaming down behind him. He was dripping wet, a puddle quickly forming around his feet.

"David?"

"Just what do you think you're doing?"

Teddy stared at David. The noose around his neck felt comfortable, like it was always meant to be there. "I'm going to the place where sunsets disappear and where sunrises cease to exist."

"That seems like a mighty far journey to take."

"Not for me it ain't."

David nodded. He furrowed his eyebrows for a moment, and then smiled big, like he always did, as if figuring something out. "But then what am I going to do?"

"What do you mean?"

"I can't very well finish the treehouse by myself now, can I?"

Teddy looked at David curiously. "No, I guess not."

"Why don't you take that rope off your neck then?"

"Because I'm tired."

"Then go to sleep."

"That's not what I meant."

"I know."

"This is easier."

David nodded again, as if understanding. He watched his friend carefully. His eyes shifted from the rope around Teddy's neck to his feet atop the bicycle seat. Teddy's face look strained and he was slightly standing on the tips of his toes, not fully on the leather seat. "No one ever said life was easy, Teddy. You have to at least try."

The words, if meant to offer comfort, stung instead. David saw Teddy's eyes flinch. He wished he could take them back, but the words had already made their mark.

"I'm done trying, David." A few tears were beginning to fall down Teddy's cheeks. "He wasn't supposed to go."

Thunder boomed again and the sky lit up behind David, and for a moment, Teddy thought David had disappeared, but then he was there again like an afterimage from a photo slowly coming into focus. Like some strange apparition appearing before his eyes, leisurely taking on flesh and blood. A ghost in the night once again returning to a body it had left behind.

Out in the rain, his father called to him, and he was ready to step forward and join him once again. One little step and he too could ride the midnight lightening. All he had to do was move his feet, not much, and it would all be over.

Pain would cease.

Life would slowly unravel like the tight cord pressed against his neck. He would breathe his last and then drift away into nothingness. A wisp of last breath then he would fade away like the smoke pouring forth from his father's mouth.

"But he did go."

"And now you're going to do the same?"

"Yes."

"But now you get to pick."

"Pick?"

"Yeah, pick. Like the little kids you told me about."

"What little kids?"

"The ones who see God too soon."

"Are you a ghost, David?"

David touched his chest with his hands. "I don't think so."

"Then an angel?"

"Can't be." He pointed to his back. "No wings."

"God's not real, David." Tears were now falling. Eyes bloodshot red like lightening. "If he was, then I wouldn't feel this way."

Words choked against the noose twisting tightly around his neck. His calves were screaming and he wanted nothing more than to let his feet slip from the bicycle seat. To take his final step from this world and to follow his father out into the black pit waiting for him on the other side.

David nodded again. He turned, looking out into the blackness that was threatening to overtake him. Consuming them both. "Then how did I know to come here tonight?"

Teddy stopped. David's words hung thick in the air. His brow furrowed and he stared at David. Eyes pleading. Rivers fell from his eyes. "David?"

"You can't go yet, Teddy."

"Why?"

"Because I still have to save you."

Thunder crashed and the sky ripped apart, a deep gash, glowing in the sky. Teddy's foot slipped. The noose tightened, digging against his throbbing jugular. He couldn't breathe. He clawed at the rope, scratching for it to come off. He was going to die the same way his father had. Hanging from the end of a rope in the middle of the garage. He wondered if his mother would follow after them as well.

When he woke, he realized he was laying on the floor of his bedroom. He could hear the patter of the rain against his window like the gentle tapping fingers of spirits roaming through the streets, searching for wayward souls finally ready to pay their fares, joining them within the dark chasm beyond their final sunset.

He stayed that way the remainder of the night. Lying on the ground next to his bed, rubbing his neck.

He didn't dream again that night, but when he closed his eyes, he could still smell smoke.

PART THREE

BEST FRIENDS AND BULLIES

CHAPTER 7

A few days passed and as Teddy quickly rode up the street to David's house, the sun was starting to set. The sky looked red and violent. Teddy's black JanSport backpack bounced back and forth as he peddled. He kept looking over his shoulder every few seconds to make sure he wasn't being followed. He hadn't seen the Belfour Three since the incident a few weeks ago, but Teddy knew it was only a matter of time before they found out where he had been going every day of the summer.

As the last of the sunset sank behind the trees, Teddy wondered how he could be so lucky to have met such a cool kid. Sure, David talked funny sometimes and dressed fancy too, but Teddy couldn't recall ever having a friend like David. It had only been three weeks since the series of unfortunate events that led to their meeting, and already Teddy felt that he had known David since kindergarten and not just for three weeks. In fact, if he hadn't decided to go out riding that day, and if the Belfour Three hadn't had chased him all across town, he probably never would have met David at all. Teddy guessed the Belfour Three were partially to thank for him meeting David in the first place. He wondered if he should perhaps thank them, smiling to himself as he turned onto the dirt path that lead up to David's house. He thought that maybe they could all sit around the firepit and sing kumbaya together, and then he laughed.

The house looked scarier at night, like a monster crouching behind the overgrown shrubbery, waiting to pounce as Teddy walked by. He parked his bike inside the garage, behind the Lincoln, like he always did, and then walked down the greying path to the backyard. His Converse made puffs of dust behind him, and a few crickets greeted him as he passed.

"What's buzzin', cousin? Did you bring them?"

"Got them right here," Teddy said, opening his backpack and showing David a bag of marshmallows, a couple Hershey chocolate bars, and a box of graham crackers.

"Swell," David smiled. He took out a box of matches and then lit the lantern he was holding. "Found this baby in the garage. I'm surprised it still works. Come on, let's go."

David led the way, the light from the lantern casting shadows that made the trees look alive. A low, deep cry came from behind them, and then a flock of birds suddenly exploded from out of the tall grass. A shudder ran down Teddy's back, and he quickly climbed the plank ladder, nailed into the tree.

The boys had furnished the inside of the treehouse with a few empty milk crates turned upside down for a table and chairs. Two sleeping bags sat rolled up in the corner, and they had hung up an old poster of Jackie Robinson that David's dad had let them have. David set the lantern down on the makeshift table while the flames danced against the walls.

"S'more time!" Teddy said, pulling the provisions from his bag and putting them next to the lantern. He grabbed a stick from off the table and jabbed a marshmallow onto the end of it.

"Wait until you see what I brought," said David, excitedly. He lifted up one of the crates and pulled a white folder out from underneath. "My dad doesn't know that I have this. He'd probably kill me if he knew that I took it outside, but I know how much you love baseball."

"No way!" Teddy squished the marshmallow he had been warming, between two crackers, melting the chocolate. He took a bite of the s'more, licked the chocolate off his fingers, and then set it down on the table. "How'd you get it?"

"My dad. He thinks that I'm an even bigger baseball nut than you are," David said, smiling as he watched Teddy take the magazine out of the folder. "And like I said, he doesn't know I took this out here, so be careful."

Teddy flipped through the pages of the magazine as if he had just been handed the keys to heaven. In his hands, he was holding "The Little Red Book of Base Ball" from 1947. David sat down on one of the crates, grinning.

"This is amazing," said Teddy. "It's got all the stats from every team. I could look at this for hours. Hey, thanks for showing this to me."

"It's yours, if you want it."

"What? No way. I couldn't."

"Sure you can."

"Wouldn't your dad be mad? I mean, he bought this for you."

"My dad is always buying me things to make up from him being gone all the time on business trips. It's fine. Besides, I want you to have it."

"Wow. Okay, thanks. I mean, only if you really don't mind. I really appreciate it."

"Don't mention it," David said, pausing before he spoke again. He watched as Teddy delicately turned another page. "Anything for my best friend."

Teddy looked up from the almanac and smiled.

"Best friends," Teddy said in agreement. The flame flickered from the lantern, as if sealing an invisible bond that had been made between the two boys. "But we were already best friends before you gave me the almanac."

David smiled.

From high above in the branches of the oak tree, an owl began to hoot, and the long grass danced in the breeze

"Anyways," David started again, leaning out the treehouse window and looking up at the full moon. "You never did tell me why those other kids were chasing you that day. We were so busy building this place, I sort of forgot that was the reason we met in the first place. Who even are the Belfour Three?"

"Brian Belfour, Jessie Cartwright, and Mike Atkins. They're eighth graders, and for whatever reason that is beyond my superior intellect, they don't like me."

"Really? I couldn't tell," David said sarcastically, still leaning on the windowsill. "The way they were chasing you and shouting that you were going to be dead meat, it looked to me that they just wanted to be friends."

"Right. Real close friends," Teddy said, punching his fist into his palm.

David chuckled.

"You know, you got to stand up to kids like that, or they won't ever quit bothering you."

"Well, the Belfour Three aren't really the kind of kids you stand up to. I think the general consensus is that you run or hide, or both."

"But you need to or you might end up like him." David came over and sat down on one of the crates and stared at Teddy. "You see, there was this kid, back where I came from, got picked on every day. It wasn't real bad, not at first, you see. At first, it was just name calling, just teasing really. Nothing too serious. They would play little pranks on him, sometimes steal his stuff and then bring it back broken or steal his knapsack for school and then return it with a dead squirrel or rat inside, but nothing too bad at first. But then it started to turn physical."

Teddy sat quietly, listening. David stared into the flame from the lantern, as if hypnotized, as he retold the story. David looked at Teddy, grey shadows dancing on his face. Then he continued.

"They pretended that they were the kid's friend, heck, they even went over to his house sometimes to play, but they were just pretending the whole time. Trying to get close to him because, for some reason, they just didn't like him. They were waiting for the perfect time to get him. And then one night, kind of like this one, his parents had him invite some of them to the house for a sleepover. They were so good at pretending, they even had the kid's parents fooled. When they were pretty sure that the kid had fallen asleep, they pulled him over to the pool inside his sleeping bag, and they threw him in. Thankfully, he was able to get out in time. It got so bad that the kid's parents had to pack up and move away. Leave their old house behind. But it turns out, the parents didn't just leave the house behind. Instead, they also left their kid behind because the kid drowned that day. Rumor has it, he still comes out at night, looking for victims to join him in the pool."

David screamed and Teddy fell backwards off the crate, landing sprawled out on the ground of the treehouse. David started laughing hysterically. Teddy, propped up on his elbows, looked at his friend angrily, and then began to laugh too.

"I wish you could have seen your face!" David laughed. As if on cue, something splashed into the pool below, and both boys screamed, throwing their arms around each other.

"There's something down there!" Teddy yelled. "It's him! It's the kid from the pool!"

"He's back from the dead!" David screamed and then began laughing again. Teddy laughed too. They stayed that way, huddled together, for part of the night before they eventually fell asleep under the moonlight.

David was sleeping. He looked like an ancient Aztec wrapped inside of a multicolored serape, ready to brave the formidable elements in the undergrowth below the treehouse and beyond, warding off evil spirits traveling through the night. Stoic and brave. A waiting totem concealed in a blanket of stars. Cocooned within the black breeze passing through the old oak tree. The low flame from the lantern danced, fire cascading down the walls of their wooden shelter. Weeping hot tears, covering David's resting face. Alternating expressions, flickering like a grinning Mexican Nagual. Changing faces like a weathered deck of cards passing between the hands of several vaqueros. Teddy could tell that David was asleep because of the slow rhythmic sound of his breath. Peaceful and relaxed. Still like stone. A granite cemetery angel resting atop a grave. Teddy, however, was fully awake. A noise from beneath the treehouse had woken him. Sleep was nowhere near his midnight horizon. He lay with his hands behind his head, tucked deep inside his sleeping bag, thoughts drifting like the grey clouds rolling overhead, too tired to grasp hold of, momentarily present then dissolving into the dark sky. Somewhere near, a coyote howled at the moon and then several others began yipping like a pack of banshees running through the waxing twilight.

He slipped out of his sleeping bag and went to the window, rubbing his arms. Leaning out, he stared at the stars overhead. Worlds like his staring back. He wondered if perhaps his father was doing the same, then quickly pushed the thought from his mind. If you dwelt on ghosts from the past for too long, especially under a moonlit sky, sometimes they had a way of making themselves known. Something flew across the sky, either a bat or an owl, he couldn't tell which, and then landed in the reaching fingers of a tree near the orange groves at the base of the surrounding hills. The trees looked like a black mass of tangles. Cancerous. Waiting to consume anything daring to travel too closely. He thought he could see a few lights flickering within, possibly kids playing a late night game of Ghosts in the

Graveyard. But then the lights disappeared and he didn't see them again.

The long grass below the treehouse swayed in the light nighttime breeze, whispering the witching hour's lullaby. The soft warm air of summer's soothing breath. Teddy heard crying from the tall weeds and a loon burst forth into the darkness, cackling as it flew away. A few crickets chirped, then grew quiet. Something was walking through the grass below. Teddy could hear the footsteps, soft and deliberate. The patient stride of a lurking creature, stalking within the shadows of the tree. The breeze slowly became whispers. Faint and raspy. Under the treehouse the Chupacabra roamed the black ground, crawling leisurely along the base of the tree, stepping over gnarled roots and tall reeds.

CHAPTER 8

When Teddy woke the next morning, sunlight was trickling in through the cracks in the wood planks, spilling onto his face. He stirred in his sleeping bag and then sat up, looking around. He grabbed a half-eaten s'more from off the table and took a bite. Chocolate smeared on his chin.

"Hey, David? Where are you?"

David was gone.

Teddy took another bite of his breakfast as he got up and looked outside the window, but he still didn't see any sign of his friend.

As he descended the plank ladder, Teddy thought he saw something or someone move behind the tall grass.

"You're not going to scare me again that easily," Teddy shouted. "I can see you hiding in the grass."

Reaching the bottom plank, Teddy suddenly felt two strong hands grab his shoulders, and he went sprawling onto his face.

"I thought I wasn't going to scare you again?" came a familiar but unwelcome voice. "I don't know? You look pretty scared to me."

Pushing himself up on his hands and knees, Teddy turned just in time to see Brian Belfour's size nine boot go flying into his stomach. Teddy fell back to the ground with a groan, and he could hear laughter coming from the tall grass.

"So, this is where you've been hiding," Brian said, grabbing Teddy by the back of the shirt and then pushing him back into the ground making Teddy taste a mixture of dirt and blood as his bottom lip split open. "I told you that you were dead meat and I always keep my word, Teddy boy."

The other two members of the Belfour Three came creeping out from behind the tall grass. Teddy quickly looked around, but he still did not see David. He began to wonder if Brian and his friends had been down there the whole night, hiding in the grass, listening to him and David talking. Teddy guessed that really didn't matter now.

"We found you, Teddy boy," laughed Jessie, as he and Mike joined Brian. They circled around Teddy, who was still lying on the ground like a wounded animal.

"Pull him up, boys!" Brian ordered and the other boys grabbed Teddy by the arms and yanked him up.

Teddy let out low moan as he felt his left shoulder pop.

"Oh, did we hurt you?" Mike asked sarcastically. "I'm sorry."

Mike punched Teddy hard in the shoulder, and Teddy cried out again. He couldn't help it, but tears were starting to run down his cheeks.

"Shut the baby up," commanded Brian, and Jessie slugged Teddy hard in the mouth.

Teddy glanced around again, looking for David, looking for a way out, but he was trapped. He was alone.

"Nowhere to run to this time, Teddy boy," said Brian, as if reading Teddy's mind. Brian stared at Teddy as if contemplating his next move, and then he smiled. "Hey, boys? Teddy looks dirty. Let's give him a bath."

Knowing what they planned to do, Teddy tried to turn and run, but they grabbed onto him and began to haul him to the pool.

"Please! No, not the pool! Please!"

Teddy tried kicking his legs. He began to twist and tried to pull away, going crazy, but his shoulder was throbbing. He managed to get one leg free and kicked out as hard as he could. Mike gave out a low groan as Teddy's left foot connected with Mike's inner thigh. Teddy slipped out of the boys' grasp, and he landed on the ground. Hard. His shoulder gave out a silent scream. He began to scramble, kicking up dirt and making a small dust storm, but Brain was able to grab Teddy and pull him back toward the group of boys.

"I told you," Brian snarled as the boys picked Teddy back up and then continued their march toward the waiting pool. "You aren't getting away this time. I hope you know how to swim because, if not, then this place is going to be your new home."

Mike and Jessie both looked at Brian, sweat dripping from both of their faces, but then quickly turned when they saw the crazy expression on their friend's face. It was one they had never seen before, and it scared them.

The boys paused at the edge of the pool; Teddy was dead weight in their arms. They all stared in awe at the water, each secretly contemplating what was going to happen next.

Except Brian.

He had already made up his mind.

Something bubbled from underneath the water, and Teddy was pretty sure that not only was there something dead under the dark green water, but there was also something living in there, as well. A faint breeze lifted the smell of death from out of the pool, and Jessie gagged, nearly dropping Teddy. But the boys all tightened their grip.

Teddy glanced around again, hoping he would see David come running out of his house to save him. Teddy looked at the tall grass, and he knew that in any second David would burst out, screaming a war cry like the savages from *The Swiss Family Robinson*.

But still, no David.

No one was coming to save him.

A tear rolled down Teddy's cheek.

"On the count of three, throw him in!" shouted Brian, almost laughing.

While Brian smiled, the other two boys looked sick. Teddy was pretty sure that Jessie was going to hurl. For a split second, Teddy thought this was all just a joke, but this was only for a second. He knew that he was going in that water. He knew that he was going to find out what was in there.

"One..." Brian yelled, and the boys began to swing Teddy. "Two..."

Teddy swung back and forth and he closed his eyes over his hot tears. Just last night, he and David were telling scary stories and eating s'mores. He tried to pretend that he was still up inside the treehouse.

"Three!" Brian shouted gleefully. The Belfour Three released Teddy and watched as he floated momentarily in the air and then came dropping with a heavy splash into the gurgling pool. Muddy water splashed in every direction.

Teddy flailed his arms. He tried to keep his head above the water. Then he went under.

The Belfour Three stood watching and laughing.

And then Brian slipped.

In his excitement of seeing Teddy sail above the pool and watching as he sank like a stone, Brian skidded across the green muck that was growing around the outer edge of the pool. Brian's arms flung behind him, his back smacked against the edge of the pool, and he slid into the murky water.

"Brian!" shouted Jessie. "We have to get him out of there. He's going to drown!"

Both boys crept to the edge of the pool, careful not to make the same mistake as their friend. Brian bobbed to the top of the water like a broken cork. He was lying face down in the water, arms spread to his sides, giving him the odd appearance of flying. Teddy splashed up beside him, gasping.

"I'm not going in there." Mike glared at Jessie. He was shaking. "It's his fault. He wanted to throw the kid in the water. Not me. He did this, not me. I'm out of here."

Mike turned and ran.

Jessie watched helplessly as his friend was tossed back and forth on the water. Teddy was struggling beside Brian, but kept going under the water.

"Something's got..." Teddy gasped as he lifted his head above the water. He swallowed a mouthful of water and then began to cough. "Something's got my foot."

And then Teddy went under the water again while Brian floated.

Jessie paced around the pool. He looked around the yard for a branch or something to grab Brian with. He found a stick and tried to pull Brian to the edge of the pool, but the stick was too short. Jessie broke the stick and then threw it in frustration.

Teddy came splashing to the surface again, making eye contact with Jessie.

"Help," Teddy said, eyes pleading. "Please."

And then he was under the water again.

The water churned like a bad dream. Jessie gave one last desperate look at the pool, and then he too turned and ran from the yard.

Teddy splashed to the surface once more. He was tired and his shoulder felt like it was on fire. He tried to grab onto Brian, to use him as support, but Teddy's hands were too slippery from the green muck that was in the pool. Each time he grabbed Brian's arm or leg, Teddy's hand slipped off or Brian would be just out of reach. He gave one last desperate attempt to grab Brian, and then Teddy sank for the last time. The treehouse loomed above like an unreachable lighthouse. Light fading in a hazy cloud of water.

Teddy was never quite sure when David got in the water. He didn't see David jump in, and he didn't hear a splash when David entered the pool. It was almost as if David was just suddenly there. Teddy felt someone free his foot from what he later found out from the police was a tree root that had grown into the pool. At first, Teddy didn't know who it was that was grabbing his foot and yanking it free. He just knew that he was no longer being pulled down under the water. Instead, he was suddenly being lifted, almost pushed, to the surface. As Teddy treaded the water, he saw David come up beside him.

"We got to get him out," Teddy said, turning to Brian. "We have to save him."

David looked at Teddy and then nodded. "Okay."

The two boys grabbed onto Brian, lifting his arms over their shoulders. They paddled him to the edge of the pool. Teddy climbed out and grabbed onto some of the grass to pull himself out, ignoring his screaming shoulder. He grabbed Brian's hands and then began to pull, David pushing Brian from behind. Teddy flopped Brian onto his back while David came crawling out of the pool, as well.

"I think he's dead," said David. He stared down at Brian, who was lying on the grass. "He doesn't look like he's breathing."

"We have to save him," said Teddy, looking at the pool. "No one deserves this."

"Okay," said David. He looked at Teddy and smiled.

Teddy dropped down beside Brian and began pressing on his chest. Even though his shoulder was throbbing louder than his heart, Teddy didn't stop until several minutes later when the police and the paramedics arrived to take over for him.

CHAPTER 9

People later called him a hero. And why wouldn't they? There was an article that ran in the city newspaper, front page, explaining how Teddy had saved Brian from drowning. The story explained how Brian had slipped into the pool, knocking himself unconscious, and how Teddy sprang into action, rescuing Brian and administering CPR until help had arrived. The article didn't mention, however, how Brian and the other two members of the Belfour Three had tried to drown Teddy first. In fact, when he was being interviewed by the police, and then again by the newspaper reporter, Teddy never once mentioned what had really happened.

If he was being honest, Teddy was still trying to figure it out himself.

When construction workers drained the pool later that week, they discovered an intricate tapestry of roots that had overtaken the bottom of the pool.

The workers also discovered what had been making the horrible smell that came from the pool. It turns out, Teddy was right when he made his assessment of the pool the first time seeing it with David, but he had underestimated himself. Along with the bundle of roots, twisted and knotted like a discarded net, the construction workers had also discovered several unfortunate small animals that had been trapped within the tree's roots. A few of the workers had gagged from the smell after draining the pool, and one even walked off the site when one of the dead animals got stuck in the drainage hose, causing the hose to burst and spraying green muck all over him.

Not long after summer ended, the long days of school started up again. Teddy began his monotonous routine of going from class to class, learning about subjects that he really couldn't care less about. However, he made some new friends. The first couple of days back, Teddy would find himself looking over his shoulder, like he always had, or peeking around corners of the school hallways, to make sure that he wasn't being followed. Teddy quickly learned, however, that his days of practicing these safety precautions were now long past. Sometimes, he would see Brian Belfour or the other two members of the Belfour Three, but they seemed to have forgotten all about Teddy, and any time their eyes did happen to meet Teddy's, they would quickly turn and head in the other direction.

Other times though, Teddy looked over his shoulder, hoping to see David. Teddy hadn't seen him since that fateful day at the pool. David had been there with Teddy, had helped

Teddy rescue Brian, but after the paramedics and the police arrived on the scene, David was gone.

As if he just disappeared.

Teddy sat on his bike, watching as the tractor and then the bulldozer rolled up the street. He'd followed from a distance and then watched as, first, David's house was torn down, then the garage, and then their treehouse. They filled the pool with dirt. All that remained after the construction crew was finished were a few wooden planks and the tire tracks from when they left.

It took them a day to tear everything down and then another day to clean out the debris. The mayor of the town wanted the place gone, and fast. In fact, at a press conference, she said that this place should have been gone fifty years ago and was surprised to see that it was still there, especially after what had happened, so many years ago.

Teddy never got the whole story, not straight out, anyway, but he was able to piece together the details from the police, the newspaper reporter, and from a little research of his own. Back in the 1940s', a family, two parents and a young boy, had lived in the house. They had been wealthy. The dad was some bigwig CEO of a company and he and the mom loved to throw parties. It was at one of these parties that their son drowned in the pool. The boy's death had been declared an accident by the police. The mother and father ended up moving to another state. They didn't even take their belongings. Instead, they just left everything behind as if the whole thing never happened. Teddy found out that both parents had died sometime in the 1950s', the mother ODing on a bottle of prescription pills and the father swallowing the barrel of a gun. The house had sat vacant since.

A forgotten tomb.

Teddy turned onto the dirt path that he'd ridden down so many times the previous month. The place felt familiar but looked different than he remembered. A few birds fluttered into the sky, disturbed by his presence. Teddy dropped his bike to the ground. There was no longer a garage or an old Lincoln to park his bike behind.

He walked to where the gate had been. The place looked smaller now that everything was gone. He glanced around, imagining the looming house, but it was hard to recall now what the house had looked like. The place was quickly becoming a vague memory. They had even knocked down the old oak tree that had held the treehouse.

Teddy walked across where the backyard would have been. The overgrown bushes and tall grass was gone. Now, there was only rocks, dirt, and a few pieces of wood scattered haphazardly around.

Walking across the yard, Teddy stopped when he felt the ground beneath his feet grow a little softer. This was where the pool had been. It felt like standing on a freshly made grave, and Teddy thought, that's exactly what it was.

He picked up a few planks of wood. Scraps remaining from the house or from the garage. Or maybe they were even pieces of the treehouse they had built together. The one they had laughed in together and told scary stories. He tied the two planks together with his father's red and white checkered hanky, and then he began to write. When he was finished, he pushed the makeshift marker into the soft soil of the makeshift grave.

Teddy stood back and looked at the wood, feeling a warm breeze pass by. The last breeze of summer perhaps.

On the grave marker, Teddy wrote:

The BEST Friend Anyone Could Ask For.
He Was Loved.

He sat that way for a while, in the dirt, watching the sunset. Pink sky mixed with swirls of blue. Fire slowly melting ice. Down the street he could see a few street lights beginning to come on. He stretched out his legs and leaned back against his forearms, something he was prone to do, and stared up at the rising stars, something else he found himself doing more of as of late. Sleepy angels blinked their eyes overhead, watching over the forgotten. Memories erased from a life moving on, a dream from another world quickly fading away like the setting sun, passing into tomorrow's eternal rest.

He wondered if he could make it, perhaps catch up to him if he pedaled hard enough, and figured he probably could, riding over the horizon to the place where there were no sunrises or sunsets, where time stood still and memories became a thing of the past because there was no longer a past, only the present moment of an eternity taking its place.

But he decided against it.

For now, this would do.

He climbed back onto his bike, sitting for a moment longer, and smiled. A land without scars from the past would be like a world without sunsets, the absence of which would forever tarnish the beauty of a rising sun.

After a moment, he turned away and rode down the dirt path for the last time. He pedaled his bike down the street, but not toward his house. Not yet anyways. Home would be waiting for him. He had made peace with that now. Instead, he pedaled down the center of the road, slowly easing his way, crisscrossing between the broken white lines painted on the street, riding toward the sunset and the prospect of tomorrow's rising sun, where summer ends.

ACKNOWLEDGEMENTS

This novella has been a journey—one rooted in memory, nostalgia, and the timeless bonds of friendship. Though fictional, it's stitched together with real emotions, echoes of youth, and fragments of moments that shaped who we become when we leave childhood behind.

I'm grateful to my wife for her patience, perspective, and quiet support throughout the process of writing this book. Her presence gave me the space and steadiness I needed to see it through from beginning to end. I've been lucky enough to share my life with you as an adult, so hopefully this book gives you some perspective into my childhood. I wrote this one for you!

To my incredible kids—thank you for reminding me daily of the joy, chaos, and wonder of growing up. Watching you discover the world in your own unique ways brought many scenes in this story to life. I hope one day you'll read this and know that the heart of this book beats with my love for you.

To the friends I grew up with—whether we're still close or we have drifted apart—you were the blueprint. Our laughter, mischief, inside jokes, and even our awkward silences are the soul of this story. I may have reimagined the faces and places, but the essence of what we shared is here.

Thanks to every mixtape, scratched CD, sleepover, late-night bike ride, and phone call that ended in static. The 90s weren't just a setting—they were a character all their own. I owe a nod to the culture, music, and weirdly wonderful energy of that era.

Finally, to the readers—thank you for taking this ride with me. I hope these pages stirred your own memories, reminded you of your own friendships, and brought back the sweetness and sting of growing up. If it made you smile or shed a tear, even once, then it was worth writing.